TWO BOYS, ONE LOVE

By

Cecil Coffey

Dedication

This story is a testament to the power of unexpected connections, the strength found in vulnerability, and the transformative potential of embracing differences. It's a celebration of the journey from animosity to acceptance, from misunderstanding to profound empathy. It's for all those who have navigated the complexities of adolescence, the challenges of self-discovery, and the sometimes painful, but ultimately rewarding process of finding your place in the world. For all those who have felt like outsiders, who have struggled to find their voice amidst the cacophony of societal expectations, who have fought to overcome internal biases and prejudices; this is for you. It's a reminder that even in the most unlikely circumstances, a detention room, a hallway, a shared moment of vulnerability, connections can be forged, bridges can be built, and understanding can blossom. For those who have known the sting of rejection, the weight of unspoken words and the sharp pain of misunderstanding, this is a story of hope, a testament to the resilience of the human spirit, and the enduring power of love in all its messy, complicated, and ultimately beautiful forms. This dedication is to quiet conversations, unspoken gestures, subtle shifts in perspective, and the enduring strength found in the most unexpected friendships. This story stands as a tribute to the moments of silent understanding, the shared smiles, and the quiet acknowledgment of a shared humanity. May it resonate with all those who have ever found solace and unexpected strength in the face of adversity, proving that even in the harshest of environments, the seeds of understanding can take root and flourish. May it inspire you to embrace your differences, celebrate your individuality, and reach out to those you might have initially perceived as adversaries. Let it be a reminder that love, in its most profound sense, is a choice, a conscious decision to see beyond the surface and embrace the complexity of the human heart.

TABLE OF CONTENTS

Chapter 1
Seeds of Discord

The air in the Northwood High hallway crackled with the usual Friday afternoon energy - a chaotic symphony of slamming lockers, hurried footsteps, and the shrill chatter of a thousand voices. Liam, a towering figure with a broad-shouldered build honed from years on the football field, navigated the throng with the effortless grace of a seasoned linebacker. His dark hair, perpetually tousled, and his confident stride announced his presence, a silent declaration of his status as one of the school's most popular athletes.

He was on a mission, a post-practice mission that involved grabbing his art supplies before heading to his dad's car for a much-needed burger. Liam wasn't particularly artistic - he viewed art class as a necessary evil to maintain his almost-perfect GPA - but he had a grudging respect for the talent of some of his classmates. He even liked how the vibrant colors of the art room brightened his otherwise monochrome athletic world.

Then he saw him.

Noah. Lean and angular, almost swallowed by an oversized hoodie that concealed the vibrant designs he often wore beneath it. Noah stood hunched over a meticulously crafted clay sculpture; his brow furrowed in concentration, a stark contrast to the vibrant energy around him. He was utterly absorbed in his work, a world away from the boisterous chaos of the hallway. Liam observed him for a moment, a flicker of curiosity bordering on grudging respect flashing across his face. Noah was undeniably talented, even if he preferred to keep to himself.

Their paths converged near the art supply cabinet. The incident began with a careless bump, Liam's shoulder accidentally knocking into Noah's, sending a cascade of colored pencils scattering across the floor. It wasn't malicious; Liam really hadn't seen him. But the reaction was immediate and explosive.

"Watch it, jock!" Noah snapped, his voice sharp, his eyes blazing with unexpected fury. The pencils were scattered, some broken, and the clay sculpture, still fragile, sat precariously on the edge of the table.

Liam, momentarily stunned by the intensity of Noah's outburst, bristled. He was used to admiration, to deference, not to this simmering anger. The anger was surprising and unwelcome.

"Hey, I'm sorry," Liam mumbled, instinctively reaching to gather the scattered pencils. His apology was clumsy, lacking the smooth, confident delivery he usually employed. This wasn't the typical response he received from those in his social circles.

"Sorry doesn't fix it," Noah retorted, his voice tight with suppressed frustration. He began gathering his own materials, his movements jerky and tense. The unspoken accusation hung heavy in the air – an accusation of carelessness, of obliviousness, of inherent privilege.

Liam stiffened. He didn't like being accused. He didn't like being made to feel like he'd done something wrong, especially when he hadn't intended to. "Look, I didn't mean to," he repeated, his voice hardening. "You were just standing there."

"Maybe if you weren't so busy flexing your muscles and bumping into people, you'd actually see where you're going," Noah shot back, his gaze meeting Liam's with a mixture of defiance and pain.

The casual cruelty was unexpected and cut deep. The words were loaded, not just a simple insult but a complex jab at Liam's athletic persona, hinting at an underlying disdain for his social status. The unspoken assumption was a common one: the popular athlete couldn't possibly care about the quiet artist. Liam had never encountered such direct, unapologetic hostility from another student.

The subtle yet intense underlying antagonism settled over the two boys. The hallway, a moment ago buzzing with the usual high school frenzy, had become their private battleground. The clash wasn't just about spilled pencils; it was a clash of worlds, personalities and deeply ingrained prejudices. It was a seed of discord, planted firmly in the fertile ground of high school anxieties and misunderstandings.

The initial exchange had been a spark; the subsequent weeks built a wildfire of animosity. Liam, fueled by a mixture of annoyance and wounded pride, found himself actively avoiding Noah. He stuck to his usual crowd, his friends reinforcing his initial disdain for the brooding artist. "He's got issues," Mark, his best friend, had declared dismissively. "Leave him alone." But the incident lingered in Liam's mind, a persistent low hum of irritation. He couldn't quite shake off the image of Noah's intense gaze, the unspoken accusation in his words, the way he'd seemed to radiate an almost palpable hurt.

Noah, on the other hand, retreated further into his shell. The incident fueled his already existing sense of alienation. He often felt like an outsider, observing the social dynamics of high school from a safe distance. Liam's casual cruelty confirmed those feelings of being invisible and deemed unimportant. He immersed himself in his artwork, pouring his anger and frustration onto canvas, finding solace in the expressive power of art. He avoided the hallways, opting for the quieter corners of the school library, a sanctuary where he could lose himself in books and sketches.

Their paths rarely crossed, yet the memory of their initial encounter remained, a phantom limb of unresolved tension. The hallway, their shared conflict space, became a stark reminder of their distinct worlds, the worlds of the popular athlete and the quiet artist, seemingly irreconcilable.

The unexpected convergence, however, came not in the bustling hallways, but in the stark, confined space of after-school detention. The small, dimly lit room reeked of stale air and regret, a space where the hushed whispers of punishment replaced the usual vibrant hum of school life. Liam, sprawled in a hard plastic chair, his usual confident posture replaced by a sullen slump, glared at the peeling paint on the wall. He was here for disrupting class _ a minor infraction, but one he regretted immediately. He had made a sarcastic comment about Coach Miller's new haircut, a comment that had somehow earned him an hour of detention.

Noah was there, too. His head bent low over a sketchbook, a quiet defiance in his posture. Liam discovered that Noah had been caught sketching in class instead of participating in the debate about the latest Marvel movie. Ironically, both were punished for acts they considered relatively minor or even justified.

The proximity was uncomfortable. The room was small, the air thick with the unspoken resentments of confined adolescents. Each boy maintained a distance, the silent tension between them far more palpable than the previous verbal sparring. This shared space, however, was now a vessel for the budding undercurrents of empathy and shared vulnerability. Liam, unexpectedly, found himself watching Noah. The intense focus on the sketchbook, the way Noah's fingers moved with practiced grace, was captivating. He'd never considered the precision and detail that went into something seemingly as simple as a drawing. The artist's quiet concentration provided a stark contrast to Liam's usual loud and boisterous nature, giving him time to notice and reflect on things other than football and his own social circle.

There was a shared discomfort, a mutual acknowledgment of their involuntary proximity. Each knew the reason for the other's presence, yet neither spoke of it. The silence was heavy, broken only by the occasional shuffle of a chair or the muted scrape of a pencil. The confined space, intended as punishment, unexpectedly became a crucible, forcing them into grudging proximity that would slowly chip away at the initial antagonism.

The confined space began to work subtly on them both. The usual loud chatter and boisterous energy of school were absent. The oppressive silence and close proximity started to loosen the initial antagonism. Liam, observing Noah's quiet intensity, felt a surprising respect. He saw the raw talent in Noah's work, a talent that existed outside the rigid boundaries of his own athletic world. He realized his previous judgements had been based solely on superficial observation of Noah's introverted demeanour and lack of participation in the superficial world of high school social life. Similarly, Noah started to notice a flicker of something akin to vulnerability beneath Liam's arrogant exterior. The brooding intensity that he initially perceived as pure arrogance started to appear less intense, more just plain shyness. The shared space of detention was becoming an unexpected arena for understanding. The foundation was laid for a reluctant but pivotal understanding.

The fluorescent lights of the detention room hummed, a monotonous counterpoint to the frantic drumming of Liam's fingers against the plastic chair. The air was stale, thick with the scent of disinfectant and regret. He glared at the peeling paint on the wall, trying to ignore the gnawing feeling of injustice. A sarcastic comment about Coach Miller's unfortunate haircut – a joke poorly received – had earned him this hour of solitary confinement. He shifted uncomfortably, the hard plastic digging into his thighs. He considered his options: sulking dramatically, which was his default setting when inconvenienced; attempting to charm the stern-faced Mrs. Davison into letting him go early, a tactic that usually worked; or simply enduring the punishment, a plan that felt particularly unappealing.

He glanced across the room. Noah. Of course. In its cruel and ironic way, the universe had decided to pair him with the source of his most recent and most unexpected conflict. Noah sat hunched over a sketchbook, his head bent low, his dark hair falling forward to obscure his face. He was a picture of quiet defiance, a stark contrast to Liam's restless energy. Liam couldn't help but notice the precision of his movements, the way his fingers danced across the page, creating something out of nothing. It was unsettling, this almost hypnotic concentration in the midst of their shared punishment.

The silence in the room was heavy, punctuated only by the occasional rustle of paper or the scratch of Noah's pencil. Liam found himself strangely captivated by this silent observation. He hadn't expected this, this forced proximity. The space was claustrophobic, and this unexpected confinement intensified the already simmering tension between them. He'd initially resented Noah's outburst, the intensity of the anger that had surprised and even shamed him. He hadn't been prepared for the raw, unfiltered emotion; he was used to carefully managed interactions and carefully constructed social dynamics. Noah, with his unexpected anger, had completely upended his usual social routine.

The initial collision of bodies, the scattered pencils, the sharp words - they formed a potent cocktail of resentment that lingered in the air. Liam's initial thoughts, a mix of annoyance and self-righteous indignation, had given way to something more complex, a grudging fascination. He couldn't deny the raw talent he saw in Noah's work, the artistic intensity that shone through his quiet, almost sullen demeanor. He had underestimated Noah's capacity to create, his raw artistic power. Liam, with his life defined by teamwork and physical prowess, had never understood the solitary pursuit of art, the internal struggle it required, the sheer dedication to an individual, quiet pursuit

He watched Noah's brow furrow in concentration. The delicate lines he was sketching seemed to hold a story, a narrative Liam was only beginning to decipher. His initial assumptions, fueled by high school social constructs and his own athletic privilege, seemed absurd in this silent, shared confinement. He suddenly understood - or rather, he was starting to understand - the subtle tension, the unspoken frustrations that fueled Noah's previous outburst.

He wondered about Noah's life outside the realm of Northwood High. Did he have friends? A family that understood his passion? Did he also feel that same frustration against the prevailing social structures in their school? Did he also feel suffocated, overwhelmed by the demands of conforming to a high school social hierarchy? Liam's own life, centered around football, had always felt relatively simple and straightforward. He understood competition, he understood teamwork, he understood the rules. But Noah's world, the world revealed in the meticulous detail of his sketches, seemed a labyrinth of emotions and experiences Liam had never considered.

Liam shifted again, the discomfort of the plastic chair suddenly unbearable. He cleared his throat, the sound echoing in the small room. The silence stretched, taut and heavy, as if waiting for something to break it. He considered speaking, offering some small acknowledgment, a nod of understanding. Yet the words eluded him. The gap between their worlds still felt vast, an unbridgeable chasm carved by years of unspoken prejudices and social expectations.

Noah, seemingly oblivious to Liam's silent contemplation, continued to work. His pencil moved with a steady rhythm, a hypnotic counterpoint to Liam's internal turmoil. Liam realized he was looking, really looking, at Noah for the first time. Not just seeing a quiet, sullen kid who was an outsider, but observing him, considering him in a new light.

The hour crawled by, each minute a small eternity. Yet, within that small space, within the confines of their shared punishment, something shifted. The initial animosity, the unspoken accusations, began to lose their potency. The shared space, intended to isolate and punish, had inadvertently created a new form of interaction, a hesitant bridge between two contrasting worlds. The seeds of understanding, planted in the soil of shared confinement and awkward proximity, began to sprout in the sterile environment of the detention room.

As the bell finally rang, signaling the end of their confinement, Liam found himself reluctant to leave. The atmosphere in the small room was oddly peaceful, a quiet truce between the athlete and the artist. The tension that had so fiercely permeated the environment had somehow softened. The shared experience had created an unexpected space for empathy, a crack in the wall of their initial antagonism. They collected their belongings, moving with a cautious awareness of the other's presence, their bodies a subtle language of shared experience and nascent understanding.

They left the detention room, walking down the hallway side by side. The usual cacophony of high school sounds seemed almost alien after the suffocating quiet of their shared confinement. Their silence now felt different, less hostile, less laden with unspoken accusations. It was a silence that spoke volumes, a silence that hinted at the potential for something new, something unexpected, something born from the unlikely proximity of an after-school detention. The seeds of understanding had been planted and despite the lingering traces of their initial conflict, there was a glimmer of hope, a faint possibility that those seeds might, one day, blossom. The hallways of Northwood High, once a battlefield, now seemed to hold the promise of a tentative reconciliation, a fragile bridge built on shared experience, and the quiet acknowledgment of a shared vulnerability.

The fluorescent lights flickered, casting long shadows across the peeling paint of the detention room walls. Liam shifted again, the uncomfortable plastic chair digging into his thighs. He'd expected the hour to be a torturous exercise in self-pity, but the reality was more... unsettling. The silence between him and Noah was thick, heavy with unspoken animosity, yet strangely... charged. He glanced at Noah, who remained hunched over his sketchbook, his dark hair a curtain shielding his face. The rhythmic scratch of his pencil was the only sound besides the hum of the fluorescent lights, a monotonous soundtrack to their shared punishment.

Liam had been stewing in his own self-righteous anger. His sarcastic comment about Coach Miller's haircut hadn't been *that* bad. He deserved detention, he conceded, but not *this* detention, not sharing this cramped, sterile space with Noah. Noah, the artistic enigma, the boy who seemed to exist in a world entirely separate from Liam's structured, athletic existence. Noah, whose unexpected outburst earlier that day still resonated, a jarring explosion of raw emotion that had caught Liam completely off guard.

Liam had always operated within a defined set of rules, a carefully constructed social landscape where he excelled. Football had provided a clear path, a predictable structure. Teammates, coaches, opponents – all part of a familiar equation. Success was measured in yards gained, touchdowns scored, victories celebrated. There was a clear hierarchy, a discernible path to achievement, and Liam thrived in it. He understood the codes, the unspoken rules of his world. But Noah's world... that was a different story altogether. A world Liam was only beginning to glimpse.

A sudden, sharp intake of breath from Noah broke the silence. Liam watched as Noah's hand flew to his chest, a stifled sob escaping his lips. Liam's initial reaction was surprise, a jolt of unexpected empathy. He'd never seen Noah display such raw vulnerability before. The image of the brooding artist, usually cloaked in quiet intensity, was shattered, replaced by a fragile, exposed human being wrestling with emotions Liam himself rarely acknowledged. He'd always assumed Noah's quiet demeanor was a sign of aloofness, a deliberate choice to remain apart from the boisterous energy of the school. But this... this was different.

Hesitantly, Liam cleared his throat. "You alright?" he asked, his voice rougher than he intended. The question hung in the air, fragile and tentative. He braced himself for Noah to dismiss him, to retreat back into his shell of silent defiance. But Noah didn't.

He slowly lowered his hand, his face still partially hidden by his dark hair. His voice was low, almost a whisper. "It's... nothing," he mumbled, but Liam sensed the lie. He saw the tremor in Noah's hand, the way his shoulders trembled slightly, betraying the attempt to maintain control. It was a vulnerability Liam hadn't expected, a glimpse into a hidden world.

A strange wave of sympathy washed over Liam. He understood the pressure, the crushing weight of expectation. He knew the relentless pressure of maintaining a carefully crafted image, the relentless striving to live up to the expectations of coaches, teammates, and the entire school. He felt the weight of it himself – the pressure to perform, succeed, never falter. But his pressure was external, visible, something he could at least attempt to control. Noah's struggle seemed... different, more internal, more private.

Liam decided to take a chance, to venture beyond the carefully constructed walls of his own comfort zone. "It's… tough, right?" he began, his voice softer now. "All the… the pressure." He hesitated, unsure of how to articulate what he was feeling, but the words flowed unexpectedly, honestly. "Everyone expects you to be... perfect. On the field, in class, all the time." He spoke about the constant pressure to perform, the fear of failure, the crushing weight of expectation that accompanied his life as a star athlete. He spoke about the isolation despite being surrounded by teammates. The pressure to conform, to fit the mold of the ideal athlete, silenced his own doubts and fears.

Noah looked up then, his eyes meeting Liam's for the first time without the veil of anger or resentment. In the dim light of the detention room, Liam saw a reflection of his own struggle, a mirror image of his internal battles. Noah nodded slowly, a single tear escaping and tracing a path down his cheek. "Yeah," he whispered, his voice catching. "It's like... you're always being watched, judged."

He spoke about his art, the constant struggle to find his voice, to express himself authentically in a world that didn't understand, or worse, dismissed it. The relentless pressure to conform to expectations, academic ones, societal ones, suffocated his artistic expression. He confessed to the isolation, the loneliness, the feeling of being an outsider, an observer, perpetually on the fringes. His voice cracked, choked with emotion, as he admitted the frustration of feeling misunderstood, of pouring his heart into his work, only to be met with indifference or ridicule.

The shared vulnerability, the raw honesty in the dimly lit detention room, was a revelation. Liam felt a genuine connection with Noah for the first time, a sense of shared understanding that transcended their initial animosity. It was a fragile connection, built on mutual understanding and an unexpected shared vulnerability, but it was there, nonetheless. The shared experience, the raw emotion, the unexpected confession created a potent bond between the star athlete and the artistic outsider. Initially, the detention room was a place of isolation and punishment, but it transformed into a space of unexpected intimacy.

The bell rang, signaling the end of their confinement, but the weight of their shared experience lingered. Liam and Noah walked out of the detention room side-by-side, their silence now different, less charged, imbued with a newfound understanding. The air between them had changed. The hostility had dissipated, replaced by something quieter, more fragile, a tentative connection forged in the crucible of shared vulnerability. The seeds of understanding, planted in the harsh soil of their shared punishment, had begun to sprout, a tiny bud of hope pushing through the hardened earth of prejudice and misconception. The hallway of Northwood High, which seemed like a battlefield moments before, now held a promise of something new, something unexpected, something born from the unlikely friendship forged within the confines of a detention room.

The hallway buzzed with the chaotic energy of students rushing between classes, starkly contrasting the quiet intensity of the detention room they'd just left. Liam and Noah walked side-by-side, a silent pact holding them together, the unspoken understanding of their shared experience hanging heavy in the air. The previous animosity, the simmering resentment, had dissipated, replaced by a hesitant, almost awkward, camaraderie. It wasn't friendship, not yet, but a tentative truce, a fragile bridge built across the chasm of their differing worlds.

That afternoon, Liam found himself inexplicably drawn to the local record store, a place he'd rarely visited before. He wasn't usually one for browsing vinyl; his time was predominantly spent on the football field or in the weight room. Still, the image of Noah sketching in the detention room, his quiet intensity a stark counterpoint to the cacophony of the school, spurred an unusual curiosity. He found himself searching for something, a connection to Noah's world, a way to bridge the gap that still existed between them.

He wasn't sure what he expected to find, but he found himself drawn to the classical section, his fingers tracing the spines of albums he barely recognised. Suddenly, he saw it – a worn copy of Beethoven's symphonies. It reminded him of the intensity in Noah's eyes, the quiet passion he'd revealed in the confession of his art. He picked up the album, turning it over in his hands, feeling an unusual sense of connection to

Noah, the artist who'd expressed his feelings with his art in the bleak detention room.

The next day, Liam saw Noah sitting alone on a bench in the park near the school, his sketchbook open, the rhythmic scratch of his pencil a familiar soundtrack to the quiet afternoon. Liam hesitated, unsure of how to approach him, the weight of his own social expectations pressing down on him. This wasn't the usual scenario. Liam's carefully structured world never involved spontaneous encounters in the park. He knew how to navigate a football game, how to execute a perfect play, but this situation was entirely unpredictable.

But something in Noah's solitary figure, his quiet concentration, compelled him to approach. Liam walked towards him, his steps hesitant, his heart beating a little faster. As he got closer, he noticed the detail in Noah's sketch, the meticulous attention to every line and curve, capturing the subtle nuances of light and shadow on the old oak tree overshadowing the park bench.

"Nice," Liam said, the word barely a whisper. He wasn't sure what else to say. He was uncomfortable, outside his comfort zone, but the words came naturally.

Noah looked up, startled, his pencil falling to the ground with a soft click. He seemed surprised, perhaps even a little apprehensive. "Oh, hey," he said, his voice low and somewhat hesitant.

There was a long, awkward silence. Liam wasn't sure how to proceed; the lack of structure or predictable rules made him uneasy. But then, surprisingly, he found himself speaking.

"I... I like Beethoven," Liam said a little sheepishly. He held his breath, waiting for a response.

Noah's eyebrows shot up, a slight smile playing at the corners of his lips. "Seriously?" he asked, a hint of surprise in his voice. "You listen to Beethoven?"

Liam nodded, feeling a sense of relief wash over him. This was unexpected common ground, a small bridge connecting their vastly different worlds. It was in that shared appreciation for music, in the quiet understanding of the beauty and power of art, that the seeds of their friendship started to take root.

They talked for a long time that afternoon about music, about art, about their dreams and frustrations. Liam learned about Noah's aspirations to become a professional illustrator, his struggles to balance his passion for art with academic pressures, the loneliness of feeling misunderstood. Noah learned about Liam's dedication to football, the constant pressure to perform, the fear of failure, and the surprisingly isolating nature of his success.

Their conversations weren't always easy. There were still awkward silences, moments of hesitant connection, and the lingering tension of their past conflict. But gradually, a sense of mutual respect and even a tentative form of friendship, began to bloom. They started meeting regularly, sometimes at the record store, other times at the park, sharing music, discussing their interests, finding a surprising resonance in their seemingly disparate lives.

One day, Liam brought a football to the park. He didn't expect Noah to be interested, but to his surprise, Noah found himself intrigued by the mechanics of the ball's spiral, the subtle nuances of Liam's throwing technique. Liam, in turn, showed a surprising level of appreciation for Noah's meticulous line drawings of the football, the precision of his sketches capturing the energy and movement of the game.

In the quiet moments, in the shared experiences, in the tentative exchanges of laughter and understanding, they discovered a remarkable connection. They found common ground not just in music but in a shared vulnerability, a recognition of the struggles of being young, navigating the pressures of expectations, and striving to find one's place in the world.

Their friendship was not an explosion of camaraderie but a slow, careful growth, a tentative budding of understanding in the rich soil of their shared experiences. Liam, the star athlete, and Noah, the artistic enigma, discovered a profound and unexpected commonality, a shared humanity that transcended the boundaries of their seemingly different worlds.

One evening, while sitting by the park, Liam found himself confiding in Noah about his concerns regarding his future. He was caught between the expectations of pursuing a professional sports career and his doubts about whether that's truly what he wanted. Noah listened patiently, offering words of encouragement and understanding. He spoke of the importance of following one's passions, of embracing the fear of failure as an inevitable part of the creative journey.

Liam listened with a newfound openness, recognising in Noah's words a reflection of his own internal struggle. He realised he'd been so focused on the external pressures, on meeting the expectations of his coaches and teammates, that he'd lost sight of his own personal aspirations and dreams. The conversation with Noah, under the soft glow of the setting sun, was a pivotal moment in his journey of self-discovery.

The budding friendship also offered Noah a much-needed support system. He shared his anxieties about an upcoming art exhibition, his concerns about the critical reception of his work. Liam, the ever-reliable star athlete, unexpectedly surprised Noah with his genuine empathy. He listened to Noah's anxieties, recognising a similar pressure within his athletic world. The pressure to achieve, to constantly excel, and the fear of failing to live up to others' expectations.

The shared vulnerability, the understanding that extended beyond the confines of their respective domains, created an unshakeable bond between them. This mutual support system, created within the nascent stages of their friendship, helped both navigate the challenges of their individual journeys with new-found resilience. This support system became their anchor, providing them with a safe space to share vulnerabilities, dreams, fears, and aspirations.

They discovered a shared appreciation for music and art as their friendship deepened. Liam started attending Noah's art classes, sketching alongside him, surprised by his own latent creative abilities. Noah, in turn, started attending Liam's football games, finding a deeper understanding of Liam's dedication and the intensity of the game, the strategic movements, the team-work. Once distinct and separate, their worlds began to inter-twine, creating a vibrant tapestry of shared experiences, mutual respect and burgeoning trust. The hesitant friendship, born in the sterile confines of a detention room, was blossoming into something far more profound, a unique connection forged in the crucible of shared vulnerabilities and unexpected empathy.

The autumn leaves crunched under their feet as they walked home from school together, a stark contrast to the sterile hall-ways and detention room that had been their initial meeting place. The air held a crispness that mirrored the growing clarity in their relationship. It wasn't just a truce anymore; a genuine warmth had begun to bloom between them, replacing the initial awkwardness with a comfortable ease. They talked about every-thing and nothing _ their favourite bands, their anxieties about upcoming exams, their dreams for the future. Liam, surprisingly articulate outside the context of the football field, revealed a thoughtful side that few had ever witnessed. Noah, in turn, showed a playful energy that hadn't been apparent in his initially reserved demeanor.

One evening, Liam invited Noah over to his house. It was an unexpected gesture, even for Liam himself. His meticulously organized, almost spartan, room was a reflection of his personality – clean lines, minimalist furniture, a single framed photo of his family on his desk. Noah, on the other hand, had always been surrounded by chaos – paint-splattered canvases, overflowing sketchbooks, and a general air of creative energy radiating from him like an aura. The contrast between their environments was as stark as their initial impressions of each other, yet within the quiet comfort of Liam's room, a different kind of energy sparked, warm and intimate.

Liam's mother, who had initially been apprehensive about her son's new friend, quickly warmed up to Noah. She saw the kindness in his eyes, the genuine respect he showed her son and the quiet intensity of his passion. She offered them both hot chocolate, observing from the kitchen doorway as they sat around Liam's small coffee table, discussing their favourite books and sharing their thoughts on the current state of the football team.

They explored each other's worlds with curiosity and respect. Liam ventured into Noah's messy art studio, initially overwhelmed by the creative chaos, but finding beauty in the intricate details of his artwork, the vibrant colours, and the raw emotion poured into every stroke. Noah, in turn, sat with Liam during his gruelling training sessions, appreciating the physical prowess and unwavering determination required for the sport. He even found himself sketching Liam in action, his lines capturing the fluidity of his movements, the intensity of his focus.

Their shared moments were interspersed with laughter - genuine, unreserved laughter that echoed their growing bond. They found humor in their differences, in the clash of their perspectives, in their shared awkwardness. They also shared moments of quiet reflection, moments where words weren't needed, where the comfortable silence spoke volumes about the trust that was blossoming between them.

Their friendship wasn't without its challenges. Liam's competitive nature sometimes clashed with Noah's more introspective personality. There were moments of misunderstanding, subtle disagreements about their respective worlds, the challenges of balancing their busy schedules. But these moments only served to strengthen their bond. They learned to communicate their feelings openly and honestly to respect their differences while celebrating their similarities. Each challenge they overcame reinforced the depth of their connection.

The external pressures of their lives loomed large, but their friendship served as a buffer, a protective shield against the storm. Liam's relentless pursuit of athletic excellence often left him feeling isolated and pressured. The weight of expectations from his family, his coach, and his teammates could be crushing. Noah provided a much-needed outlet, a safe space where Liam could vent his frustrations, where he could be simply Liam, not the star athlete.

Similarly, Noah's passion for art was met with skepticism from some, who saw it as an unrealistic pursuit, an impractical way to earn a living. He grappled with self-doubt, struggling to balance his creativity with the demands of academics. Liam's unwavering support, his unwavering belief in Noah's talent, gave him the strength to persevere, to ignore the naysayers and follow his heart.

One day, while sitting by the lake near Noah's house amidst a serene, peaceful landscape, Liam shared a deep-seated fear: the fear of failure. Not just in football, but in life. The fear of not living up to his potential, of not achieving everything he felt he should, of letting down those who believed in him. He'd never shared these insecurities with anyone before. Noah listened patiently, his eyes full of empathy. He spoke of his own fears, his own doubts, the vulnerability of putting his art on display for the world to see.

This shared vulnerability created an even stronger bond between them. It was in their shared anxieties, in their shared struggles, that they found the deepest connection, a resonance that went far beyond their initial differences. Their friendship became a sanctuary, a place where they could be themselves, without judgment or pretense.

Liam's visit to Noah's home revealed a different side of Noah, too. His family, initially perceived as distant and cold by Liam, welcomed him with warmth, understanding the depth of his friendship with their son. The simple act of sharing a meal together, listening to music, engaging in lighthearted banter, fostered an atmosphere of acceptance. Liam discovered a strong sense of family unity and realized Noah's art's profound impact on his family, bringing them closer through shared appreciation and joy.

The transformation extended beyond their personal lives. Liam's presence at Noah's art exhibition was a quiet but powerful gesture. He'd never attended an art exhibition before, but he wanted to be there for Noah to support his friend's dream. Noah, in turn, attended Liam's football games with a new understanding, appreciating the teamwork, the dedication, the pressure, and the sheer joy of competition that Liam displayed. Their different worlds were no longer distinct entities; they'd become intertwined, enriching each other, expanding their horizons.

Their friendship became an unexpected masterpiece, a testament to their ability to bridge their differences to appreciate the beauty in each other's unique worlds. It was a quiet revolution, a transformation born in a detention room, nurtured in shared laughter, strengthened in moments of vulnerability, and blossoming into a deep and abiding connection that would shape the trajectory of their lives in ways neither could have predicted. The seeds of discord, planted in their initial conflict, had yielded a harvest far richer and more unexpected than either could have imagined. Their friendship wasn't just a bond; it was a testament to the power of understanding, empathy, and the unexpected connections that blossom in the most unlikely of places.

Chapter 2
Navigating Societal Pressures

The whispers started subtly, like the rustling of leaves before a storm. At first, Liam and Noah barely registered them. They were too absorbed in their burgeoning friendship, in the shared laughter, the quiet understanding, the unspoken comfort they found in each other's company. But the whispers grew louder, more insistent, weaving themselves into the fabric of their school days, seeping into the spaces between classes, echoing in the hallways.

It began with curious glances, then sideways smiles, followed by pointed remarks. Liam, the star quarterback, was seen with *Noah*, the brooding art kid, a boy who kept to himself, a boy who wasn't part of the "in-crowd." The dissonance was jarring, a stark contrast that didn't fit the pre-defined social landscape of their high school. Liam's usual camaraderie with the football team took on a subtle edge. His teammates, initially accepting, started to distance themselves, their playful banter replaced by uneasy silences and pointed questions. "What's going on with you and...*him*?" The unspoken implication hung heavy in the air, a judgment wrapped in casual inquiry.

The pressure wasn't limited to the football field. The usual boisterous lunch breaks in the school cafeteria became punctuated by hushed conversations as Liam and Noah sat together, a clear anomaly in the established social order. Liam, used to the spotlight, found himself the target of curious and occasionally hostile, stares. He'd been a symbol of athletic prowess, a figure of admiration. Now, his association with Noah seemed to taint his previously flawless image. He felt the shift, the subtle rejection, the silent disapproval.

Noah, accustomed to his own quiet solitude, found the scrutiny even more intense. His art, once a refuge, now felt exposed, vulnerable. The whispers followed him from classroom to classroom, transforming his work into a subject of discussion, often laced with disdain. His quiet demeanor was misinterpreted as arrogance, his passion for art deemed "weird," "unrealistic," and "pointless." He found himself retreating further into himself, the vibrant colors of his paintings seeming to dim under the weight of the judgment.

Family dinners became tense affairs. Liam's parents, initially pleased by Noah's positive influence on their son, began to notice the subtle shifts in their son's social dynamics. The once-easy conversations around the dinner table were replaced by awkward silences punctuated by uneasy glances between Liam and his father. Liam's father, a man of tradition and rigid expectations, struggled to understand the nature of his son's friendship with Noah. He saw it as a distraction, a deviation from the path of athletic excellence, a potential threat to Liam's future. His subtle disapproval created a palpable tension in the room, casting a shadow over their shared meals.

Similar tensions arose in Noah's home. While his family was more accepting of his friendship with Liam, their initial enthusiasm waned as they observed the increasing social scrutiny. His mother, a woman of quiet strength, tried to remain supportive, but couldn't ignore the whispers circulating through their close-knit community. The subtle disapproval from some community members and the unspoken judgments created a ripple effect, adding to the pressure Noah already felt.

The social gatherings, once opportunities for connection and shared experiences, transformed into minefields of subtle judgments and awkward encounters. At a school dance, Liam and Noah found themselves on the periphery, watching the familiar cliques intertwine, their space increasingly isolated. The casual conversations drifted away, replaced by pointed remarks and condescending smiles. They were seen as outsiders, not part of the established social fabric.

Teachers, too, observed the shifting dynamics, sensing the tension between Liam and Noah and their peers. Some tried to intervene subtly, offering words of encouragement, reminding them of the importance of staying true to themselves. Others, however, inadvertently added to the pressure, their unspoken biases seeping into their interactions. The school, a place of learning and community, felt more like a battleground.

Liam and Noah navigated these turbulent waters with varying degrees of success. Liam, fueled by his competitive spirit, initially tried to ignore the whispers to maintain the status quo. He continued to spend time with Noah, but found himself withdrawing from the football team, feeling increasingly isolated. The weight of expectation, coupled with the social pressure, took its toll. His usually cheerful demeanor became strained, his confident smile replaced by a tight-lipped reserve.

Noah, on the other hand, reacted to the scrutiny by retreating further into his art. He channeled his frustrations and anxieties into his work, pouring his emotions onto canvases, transforming his vulnerabilities into vibrant expressions of pain, resilience, and hope. His art became his shield, a way to process the negativity, to assert his identity against the tide of disapproval.

The external pressure tested their friendship, threatening to unravel the fragile threads of their connection. There were arguments, misunderstandings, moments of doubt. Liam questioned whether their friendship was worth the social cost, the alienation, the scrutiny. Noah grappled with his own insecurities, wondering if his art, and by extension, his friendship with Liam, was truly worth the ridicule. They navigated their internal struggles alongside the external pressures, their love and support for each other acting as an anchor in the stormy seas.

One evening, after a particularly brutal day at school, Liam and Noah found themselves sitting by the lake, the moon casting a silvery glow on the water. The silence, once a comfortable companion, was now heavy with unspoken anxieties. Liam confessed his fears, the vulnerability he hadn't shown even to his own family. He spoke about the pressure to conform, to meet the expectations of his peers, of his family, of his coach. He admitted feeling isolated, alone, trapped within the confines of his public image.

Noah listened, his understanding eyes mirroring Liam's anxieties. He shared his own struggles, his own vulnerability, the constant battle against self-doubt and the pressures of artistic expression. He talked about the pain of facing rejection, the fear of failure, the constant need to prove himself.

In that moment of shared vulnerability amidst the stillness of the night, their friendship deepened. They found solace in their shared anxieties, their shared struggles. They realized that the external pressures, though intense, couldn't diminish the bond they had forged. Their friendship wasn't about conformity; it was about acceptance, understanding, and the courage to be themselves, regardless of the consequences. The external world could judge them, but their friendship remained their sanctuary, a haven from the storm. The whispers still echoed in the hallways, but within the walls of their friendship, a quiet resilience bloomed, a testament to the power of love in the face of adversity. Their relationship, once a subject of hushed conversations and sidelong glances, was now a silent affirmation of their own strength, their own unwavering commitment to each other. And that was a strength that resonated far beyond the reach of any social scrutiny.

Liam lay in his bed, the darkness a comforting blanket against the relentless buzz of his thoughts. The whispers, the sideways glances, the subtle distancing of his teammates – they weren't just external pressures; they'd burrowed their way inside him, creating a discordant symphony of doubt and uncertainty. He'd always been the star quarterback, the golden boy, the epitome of athletic success. Now, that carefully constructed image felt fragile, threatened by his friendship with Noah. Was he betraying his team? Was he throwing away his future?

He closed his eyes, picturing his father's disappointed face at the dinner table. The unspoken disapproval had been heavy, a silent judgment that resonated far louder than any shouted accusation. His father's expectations were ingrained in Liam's very being, the blueprint for his success, his future. And now, Noah seemed to be disrupting that carefully laid plan with his quiet intensity and unconventional passions. Was his friendship with Noah a betrayal of his father's hopes and dreams? A reckless deviation from the expected path?

The guilt gnawed at him. He loved Noah's company, the ease of their communication, the way Noah saw him, not as the star quarterback, but as Liam, a person with flaws and vulnerabilities. Yet, the constant pressure to conform, to adhere to the rigid social norms of their high school, was almost unbearable. He was trapped between two worlds: the world of expectation and the world of his heart.

Noah, meanwhile, sat alone on a park bench, sketching in his worn leather-bound journal. The vibrant colors of his art were usually his solace, his escape from the world's harsh realities. But today, the colors felt muted, as if reflecting the grayness of his own conflicted emotions. The whispers hadn't just targeted Liam; they'd reached him, too, turning his passion into a source of anxiety and self-doubt.

He'd always been the "art kid," the outsider, the one who preferred the company of canvases and brushes to the boisterous energy of the football field. He was used to solitude, but the scrutiny, the feeling of being judged and misunderstood, was a new kind of pain. Had he made a mistake? Had his friendship with Liam brought unwanted attention, unwanted scrutiny? The thought sent a shiver down his spine. Had he inadvertently dragged Liam into the vortex of his own quiet isolation?

His art had always been his refuge, his sanctuary. Now, it felt like an open wound, exposed to the judgment of others. He longed for acceptance, not just from his peers, but from himself. He struggled to reconcile the vibrant, expressive side of himself, so clearly evident in his art, with the quiet, withdrawn persona he presented to the world. He felt torn between embracing his true self and conforming to expectations, between his passion and the fear of judgment.

As they walked home from school one evening, a rare silence hung between them. The usual easy flow of conversation was replaced by an unspoken tension. Liam finally broke the silence. "I... I've been thinking a lot lately," he began, his voice barely above a whisper. "About everything."

Noah nodded, his eyes searching Liam's face. He knew what was coming.

Liam continued, his words hesitant at first, gaining momentum as he confessed his anxieties and internal turmoil. He admitted his fear of losing his friends, of disappointing his parents, of jeopardizing his future. He felt trapped, caught in a web of expectations, his identity threatened by the social pressure to conform. He wasn't just wrestling with the external pressures but battling his internal demons.

Noah listened patiently, his heart aching for his friend. He understood Liam's fears; they echoed his own anxieties. He confessed his own internal struggles, his own self-doubt. He spoke of the constant pressure to prove himself, the feeling of being an outsider, the fear of never truly belonging.

They found solace in their shared vulnerability, in the understanding that their struggles weren't unique, that they weren't alone in their battles. They sat on a park bench, the late afternoon sun casting long shadows around them. It was a moment of profound connection, a testament to their friendship's resilience.

The conversation opened the door to further introspection. Liam found himself examining his own values. Was athletic success the only measure of his worth? Was conforming to societal expectations the only path to happiness? He began to question the rigid definitions of masculinity that had been imposed upon him, acknowledging the vulnerability and sensitivity he'd previously suppressed.

Noah, too, delved deeper into his own identity. He challenged the idea that his art needed to be validated by others to hold worth. His passion, his self-expression, was not contingent on external approval. He began to realize that his quiet strength and artistic expression were integral parts of who he was, regardless of external perception.

In the ensuing weeks, Liam and Noah embarked on a journey of self-discovery. They supported each other, holding each other accountable to their own values. Liam found himself becoming more assertive, communicating his feelings to his parents and teammates, although the conversations were not easy. He found a new sense of purpose in his athletic career, not solely focused on external validation but also on personal growth and teamwork. He embraced his role as a role model, challenging traditional expectations of masculinity and proving that strength could come in many forms, including vulnerability.

Noah, too, showed more courage, exhibiting his art in a local gallery despite his initial apprehension. The feedback was mixed, as expected, but he learned to value the genuine response over the superficial praise, celebrating the people who truly appreciated his work. He actively sought out other creative individuals, forming bonds with others who understood the pressures and rewards of artistic pursuits.

Their journey wasn't without its setbacks. There were moments of doubt, times when the external pressures felt insurmountable. But their shared vulnerability, their mutual support, and their growing self-awareness strengthened their bond. Their friendship became a sanctuary, a haven where they could be themselves, flaws and all. The internal conflicts didn't vanish entirely, but they learned to manage them, to navigate the complexities of their evolving feelings, and to celebrate the strength they found within themselves and within each other. They transformed their internal struggles into sources of strength and resilience, proving that even in the midst of societal pressure and personal turmoil, authentic connections and self-acceptance could thrive. Their story became a testament to the power of love, friendship, and the courage to be true to oneself, regardless of the consequences.

The weight of unspoken expectations continued to press down on Liam, even after his heart-to-heart with Noah. He felt a constant low-level hum of anxiety, a background noise to his life that he couldn't quite silence. Even his successes on the football field felt tainted, overshadowed by the internal conflict raging within him. The cheers of the crowd seemed to blend with the whispers of doubt, a disconcerting mix of praise and condemnation.

He found himself seeking out Mrs. Rodriguez, his guidance counselor, a woman known for her quiet wisdom and her uncanny ability to listen without judgment. Her office, a small but calming space tucked away in a corner of the school, became a refuge for him. The aroma of chamomile tea, a constant presence in her room, helped soothe his frayed nerves.

He sat across from her, the worn wooden desk a silent witness to countless confessions and anxieties. He started hesitantly, stumbling over his words, unsure of how to articulate the turmoil within. He spoke about the pressure from his father, the expectations of his teammates, the fear of letting everyone down. He confessed his feelings for Noah, the joy and the fear that came with it, the way it threatened to unravel everything he thought he knew about himself and his future.

Mrs. Rodriguez listened patiently, her eyes filled with a gentle understanding. She didn't offer quick fixes or easy answers. Instead, she asked insightful questions, guiding him to explore his own feelings, to unravel the tangled threads of his anxieties. She helped him to see that his feelings weren't abnormal, that his struggles were a shared human experience, and that there was no shame in feeling overwhelmed.

"Liam," she said softly, her voice a calm counterpoint to the storm raging inside him, "It's okay to feel conflicted. It's okay to not have all the answers. What truly matters is that you're honest with yourself, that you're trying to understand your own values and priorities."

She helped him to articulate the core of his conflict: the clash between his internal compass and the external pressures he faced. She challenged him to examine the source of his self-worth to question whether athletic achievement should be the sole measure of his value. She helped him realize that his identity wasn't solely defined by his role as a star quarterback. He was a son, a friend, a person with his own unique passions and dreams _ a whole person beyond the football field.

Noah, too, found support in an unexpected place _ Mr. Evans, the aging art teacher, a man with a kind heart and a mischievous twinkle in his eye. Mr. Evans had seen countless students struggle with the same anxieties Noah faced, the fear of judgment, the pressure to conform, the struggle to reconcile their artistic passions with the demands of a world that didn't always value creativity.

Their conversations usually took place after school, in Mr. Evans' cluttered studio, amidst canvases, brushes, and the scent of turpentine. The studio, with its walls adorned with vibrant paintings and sketches, was a world away from the sterile corridors of the school, a place where self-expression was not only tolerated but celebrated. Mr. Evans listened to Noah's anxieties, his doubts, and his fears with empathetic patience.

"Noah," he'd say, his voice gravelly but reassuring, "Art is about vulnerability. It's about laying your soul bare, about showing the world who you truly are. And that takes courage. Don't let the fear of judgment silence your voice, your passion."

He helped Noah understand that the value of his art wasn't determined by external validation. He reminded him that his art was a reflection of his inner world, a testament to his unique perspective, and that its worth resided in its authenticity, not its

popularity. He encouraged Noah to share his art, to connect with
other artists, to find his artistic community _ a group of like-
minded individuals who understood his struggles and celebrated his triumphs.

Mr. Evans also helped Noah to confront his own insecurities. He encouraged him to view criticism not as a personal attack but as an opportunity for growth, a chance to refine his
craft, to deepen his understanding of his art. He helped him realize that self-doubt was a natural part of the creative process,
but that it shouldn't paralyze him. He urged Noah to embrace
his unique style, celebrate his individuality, and trust his creative instincts.

Liam and Noah found solace in sharing their experiences
with each other, their vulnerabilities becoming a bridge to
deeper understanding and mutual support. They talked openly
about their fears, their hopes, and their dreams, their conversations often stretching into the late hours of the night. They found
strength in each other's resilience, inspiration in each other's perseverance.

Liam learned to appreciate Noah's quiet strength, his unwavering commitment to his art, his ability to find beauty in the
mundane. He saw the courage it took for Noah to express himself authentically, even in the face of potential rejection. Noah,
in turn, learned to appreciate Liam's sensitivity, his capacity for
empathy, his willingness to challenge societal expectations. He
saw the strength Liam possessed beneath the veneer of athletic
prowess, his capacity for vulnerability, his genuine goodness.

Their mutual support extended beyond their personal struggles. They became each other's advocates and champions of each other's dreams. Liam supported Noah in showcasing his art in local galleries, celebrating his artistic successes. Noah, in turn, supported Liam in navigating the challenges of his athletic career, reminding him to focus on his personal growth, value his relationships, and live a life authentic to himself.

Their journey wasn't always easy. There were moments of doubt, setbacks, and internal conflict. But their shared experiences, their mutual support, and the guidance of their mentors, helped them to navigate these challenges with grace and resilience. They learned that true strength lies not just in athletic prowess or artistic talent, but in the courage to be oneself, to embrace one's vulnerabilities, and to forge authentic connections with those who truly understand and appreciate us. They learned that societal pressures can be overwhelming, but the support of true friends, mentors, and self-acceptance can help to navigate those challenging waters, creating a path towards self-discovery and fulfillment. Their friendship, once a source of anxiety, had become their greatest strength, a beacon of hope in a world that often felt overwhelming and judgmental. They had found their haven, not just in their shared vulnerability, but in the resilience of their bond, and the unwavering support of those who believed in them.

The Friday night game loomed, a behemoth casting a long shadow over Liam's week. The pressure was suffocating, a relentless tide threatening to pull him under. He'd excelled all season, his throws precise, his leadership unwavering, yet the constant undercurrent of his father's expectations – the unspoken demand for a football scholarship, a path to a life Liam wasn't sure he wanted, gnawed at his peace. Even Noah's unwavering support felt like a fragile shield against the storm.

He found himself practicing extra hard, pushing his body to its limits, a desperate attempt to silence the inner critic. But the harder he pushed, the more exhausted he became, both physically and emotionally. The cheers of the crowd, once a source of exhilaration, now sounded hollow, a reminder of the performance he was expected to deliver, a performance that felt increasingly disconnected from his true self.

The confrontation with his father came during a tense dinner, the air thick with unspoken resentments. Liam's father, a man of few words but immense expectations, broached the subject of college applications, his voice tight with suppressed emotion. He spoke of prestigious universities, of scholarship offers, of a future meticulously planned, a future that didn't include art schools or anything that didn't involve a football field.

Liam finally spoke his truth, emboldened by his conversations with Mrs. Rodriguez and the strength he found in his friendship with Noah. He explained his feelings about football, the weight of expectation, his desire to explore his own passions, even mentioning his relationship with Noah, a revelation met with stunned silence. The ensuing argument was difficult, raw, and deeply emotional, a clash between two worlds, two visions of the future. But for the first time, Liam felt a sense of liberation, a release from the burden of unspoken expectations. The fight wasn't easy, leaving a lingering tension in their relationship, but it paved the way for a different kind of understanding, a beginning of open communication.

Meanwhile, Noah faced his own battles. He had submitted his portfolio to a prestigious art competition, a significant step in his artistic journey. The anticipation was agonizing, the fear of rejection a constant companion. The judgment of others and the possibility of failure weighed heavily on him, threatening to eclipse his creative passion. He found solace in Mr. Evans' studio, the vibrant colors and textures a soothing balm against the anxieties that plagued him.

He spent hours working on a new piece, pouring his emotions onto the canvas, translating his anxieties, his hopes, his dreams into a visual language. The process was cathartic, a way of processing his feelings, of giving form to his inner turmoil. The finished piece, a bold and emotionally charged expression of his journey, became a testament to his resilience, his unwavering dedication to his art.

The competition results arrived like a thunderbolt. Noah's piece had won, a testament to his talent, his dedication, and his courage. The win was not just a personal triumph; it was a validation of his artistic vision, a validation of his authenticity. He celebrated with Mr. Evans; the elation tempered with a quiet sense of gratitude for the support and guidance he had received. The win wasn't just about the prize; it was about the recognition of his journey, his struggle, his growth.

The acceptance of his art extended beyond the confines of the competition. Local galleries showed interest, offering exhibition opportunities. His art, once a source of anxiety, now became a means of connection, a way to express himself and reach out to others. He started sharing his work online, connecting with other artists, building a community that understood and appreciated his art.

Liam and Noah's support for each other remained unwavering. Liam attended Noah's gallery opening, witnessing the admiration and appreciation for his friend's work. He felt a swell of pride, not just in Noah's accomplishment, but in their shared journey. Noah, in turn, supported Liam, attending his games, offering encouragement and understanding during the intense pressure of the season. He reminded Liam to focus on his own well-being, to value his friendships, and to live a life that felt authentic to him.

The final game of the season arrived, the weight of expectations still present, but less oppressive. Liam played with a new-found freedom, a sense of liberation that came from embracing his true self. The performance was magnificent, his throws precise and powerful, his leadership inspirational. But the victory, while exhilarating, wasn't the sole focus. The game became a testament to his personal growth, a celebration of his journey towards self-acceptance.

The season ended with Liam's announcement that he would not be pursuing a football scholarship, a decision that initially shocked his father but ultimately resulted in a shift in their relationship. His father, realizing Liam's unwavering determination and the support of his son's friend and art teacher, began to understand and appreciate his son's artistic vision. The path ahead was uncertain but filled with a newfound sense of hope and possibility.

Liam applied to an art school, a decision that represented a significant departure from his family's expectations, but a leap towards his true self. He knew there would be challenges ahead, that the path wouldn't be easy, but he had the unwavering support of Noah, his friends, and his mentors. He had learned that true strength wasn't defined by athletic prowess or adherence to societal norms, but by the courage to embrace one's true self and to forge one's own path.

The summer following their senior year was filled with preparation for their respective futures. Noah, brimming with confidence and artistic direction, spent his days refining his technique and connecting with other artists. Liam, inspired by Noah's artistic journey, immersed himself in art-related studies, discovering a hidden passion he never knew existed. They continued to support each other, their friendship a cornerstone of their individual journeys.

They navigated challenges; there were moments of doubt and uncertainty. Liam's father, initially resistant to his change in plans, eventually came to terms with his son's decision and provided begrudging but heartfelt support. Noah faced setbacks in

his artistic pursuits, learning to navigate the criticisms and rejec-
tions with grace and resilience. They learned that life wasn't a
straight line; it was a winding path with bumps and curves, but
with the support of their mentors and each other, they were able
to navigate the uncertainty.

Through it all, their friendship deepened, becoming a resilient and unwavering force. Their vulnerabilities, once sources of
anxiety, transformed into pillars of strength. Their shared experiences forged a bond of mutual understanding and unwavering
support, a testament to their friendship's resilience and commitment to self-discovery. They had overcome societal pressures
not by conforming, but by embracing their authentic selves, a
testament to their individual strength and the profound power
of their shared journey. They had proven that true success lay
not in meeting external expectations, but in embracing internal
truth.

The curtain fell on the school play, a wave of applause washing over the stage. Liam, backstage, felt a surge of pride, not just
for the successful performance but for Noah, whose set design
had transformed the auditorium into a breathtaking dream-
scape. The vibrant colors, the intricate details, the sheer artistry
of it all – it was a testament to Noah's talent and dedication. He
found Noah amidst the post-show chaos, a whirlwind of con-
gratulations and hugs swirling around him. Noah, usually reserved, beamed with an infectious joy, his eyes shining with a
light Liam had rarely seen before. That night, under the glow of
the stage lights and the celebratory chatter, their bond felt
stronger than ever, solidified by shared triumph.

Liam's own victory on the football field a few weeks later felt different this time. The pressure was still there, the expectations still weighed heavily, but there was a newfound lightness in his stride, a sense of freedom he hadn't felt before. He played not just for the team, not just for his father, but for himself, for Noah, for the validation of his own journey. After the game, surrounded by cheering teammates, he saw Noah in the stands, his face alight with pride and support. Their shared glance transcended the roar of the crowd, a silent acknowledgement of their mutual journey, their mutual strength. That night, victory felt sweeter, shared not just with his team, but with his closest friend.

The turning point, however, came unexpectedly during a family Thanksgiving dinner. Liam's father, still grappling with his son's decision to pursue art instead of football, had been distant and reserved. The tension hung heavy in the air, a palpable silence that threatened to suffocate the celebratory mood. Then, Noah arrived, armed with a beautifully wrapped sketchbook, a gift for Liam's father containing original sketches depicting scenes from Liam's football games. The sketches were both powerful and moving, capturing the intensity and spirit of Liam's performance on the field with incredible skill and passion. Liam's father, a man of few words, was visibly touched. He examined the sketches, his stoic expression slowly softening, replaced with a glimmer of understanding and appreciation. A hesitant smile touched his lips. He acknowledged Noah's gift, thanking him in a low, heartfelt tone, and for the first time, he looked directly at Liam with a newfound respect, finally appreciating Liam's commitment and genuine passion.

The acceptance wasn't immediate, nor was it perfect. There were still moments of awkwardness, remnants of unspoken expectations lingering between Liam and his father. But the night served as a pivotal moment, a bridge across the chasm that had separated them. It showcased not only Noah's artistic talent but also his empathy and understanding. He had, in essence, facilitated a crucial step in Liam's reconciliation with his father, demonstrating the profound power of art and friendship in bridging divides.

The following months saw Liam and Noah navigating the complexities of their respective futures. Liam applied to art school, his portfolio a testament to his newfound passion, infused with the support and inspiration he found in Noah's artistic journey. The acceptance letter arrived like a beacon, illuminating a path toward self-discovery and creative freedom. Noah, meanwhile, saw his artistic work blossom. Local galleries embraced his unique style, offering exhibitions and opportunities that exceeded his wildest dreams. His art, once a source of anxiety, transformed into a source of connection and fulfillment.

Throughout this whirlwind of change, their friendship remained their unwavering anchor. They celebrated each other's triumphs, offered comfort during setbacks, and shared in life's everyday moments. The shared experiences, late-night studio sessions, early morning football practices, hushed conversations under the starry sky, deepened their bond, transforming their

vulnerabilities into shared strength. They were not just friends;
they were fellow travelers on a journey of self-discovery, their
companionship an unwavering source of support and inspiration.

Their connection extended beyond their personal triumphs
and struggles. They found themselves involved in community
projects, collaborating on murals for local schools, participating
in fundraising events for various causes. Their collaboration,
seamlessly weaving together Liam's drive and leadership with
Noah's artistic vision, became a force for positive change within
their community. Their work captured the essence of their
friendship, a blend of dynamism and creativity, strength and resilience. They were no longer just individuals striving for personal success; they were a team, supporting each other, inspiring
each other, and making a difference together.

The challenges they faced, Liam's father's initial resistance,
Noah's anxieties surrounding his art, became mere stepping
stones on their path to growth. They learned that adversity was-
n't something to be feared, but a catalyst for resilience, for
deeper understanding, for a stronger bond. They learned to lean
on each other, to support each other's dreams, and to celebrate
each other's strengths.

One particular evening, as they sat by the lake, reflecting on
their journey, the full weight of their shared experience settled
upon them. The lake, a tranquil mirror reflecting the twilight
sky, seemed to symbolize the quiet strength of their friendship.
Liam expressed his gratitude for Noah's unwavering support

and willingness to stand by him despite societal pressures and family expectations. Noah, in turn, expressed his appreciation for Liam's understanding, his genuine admiration for Noah's art, and his belief in his talent. Their hushed and sincere conversation encapsulated the profound depth of their connection, a bond forged in mutual respect, unwavering support, and shared resilience.

The summer before college, they spent countless hours together, working on a final collaborative project, a series of paintings celebrating the resilience of the human spirit. The paintings, a powerful visual representation of their journey, captured the strength of their friendship, their unwavering support for each other's dreams, and their shared triumph over societal pressures. Their art became a testament to the enduring power of their bond, a beacon of hope, a celebration of authenticity, and a validation of their unique journey.

As they stood on the precipice of their individual futures, Liam and Noah knew that their journey was far from over. They knew there would be new challenges, new hurdles to overcome, but they also knew they wouldn't face them alone. Their friendship, forged in adversity, honed by shared triumphs, and strengthened by mutual respect, would continue to serve as an unwavering anchor, a beacon of hope, and a constant source of inspiration, guiding them on their individual paths while ensuring that their bond remained as strong as ever. They had proven that true strength wasn't about conforming to expectations, but about embracing one's authentic self and that true success lay not in external validation but in the unwavering support of a true friend. The strength of their bond became a symbol of their individual strengths, a testament to the power of friendship in navigating life's complexities and achieving one's truest potential.

Chapter 3
Acceptance and Understanding

The following Christmas was a watershed moment. Liam's mother, ever perceptive, had noticed the subtle shift in her husband's demeanor towards Liam. She'd seen the quiet moments of shared glances between Liam and his father, the hesitant smiles, the unspoken acknowledgment of a growing understanding. She'd also observed the genuine warmth her husband showed towards Noah, a warmth that extended beyond mere politeness. This year, she orchestrated a family gathering that felt different, deliberate. It was less about forced tradition and more about genuine connection.

Noah arrived, carrying a beautifully crafted wooden bird, a small sculpture intricately detailed, a testament to his evolving artistic skills. He presented it to Liam's father, a gesture that was both simple and profoundly meaningful. There was no grand speech, no dramatic unveiling, just a quiet offering of a carefully chosen gift, a symbol of his appreciation and respect. Liam's father, his eyes crinkling at the corners, accepted the gift with a quiet gratitude that spoke volumes. He placed the bird on the mantelpiece, its elegant form a silent witness to a changing dynamic within the family.

The dinner itself was a revelation. The usual tense silences were replaced by easy conversation, laughter, and genuine engagement. Liam's father, encouraged by his wife's subtle nudges and the warmth radiating from Noah's quiet presence, engaged Liam in a conversation about his art school application, his tone laced with genuine interest, not the previous skeptical undercurrent. He asked about Liam's projects, his aspirations and listened intently to Liam's passionate responses. He even offered a thoughtful opinion on one of Liam's sketches, his words carefully chosen, revealing a newfound respect for Liam's creative endeavors.

The conversation flowed naturally, the initial awkwardness dissipating with each shared moment, each exchanged a smile and each shared laugh. It wasn't a sudden transformation, but a slow, organic process of acceptance, a gradual thawing of the icy reserve that had once separated them. Noah, with his quiet charm and genuine warmth, played a pivotal role in bridging the gap between father and son, fostering an environment of mutual respect and understanding.

Later that evening, as the family gathered around the fireplace, Liam's father pulled Liam aside for a private conversation. It was a quiet, unassuming talk, devoid of grand pronouncements or dramatic confessions. It was simply a father acknowledging his son's choices, his passions, and his dreams. He admitted that he'd been wrong, that his preconceived notions about art and success had blinded him to the beauty and talent residing in his son's heart. He confessed that seeing Noah's genuine respect for Liam's passion had opened his eyes, and his understanding of Liam and his art had grown. He expressed his pride in Liam's courage to pursue his own path, his own passion.

Liam, overwhelmed by his father's words, felt a surge of emotion, a mixture of relief, gratitude, and profound love. He spoke of his journey, his struggles, and his newfound confidence. He thanked his father for finally seeing him, for understanding his choices. The words flowed freely, unburdened by the years of unspoken expectations and unspoken resentments. Their embrace, a simple gesture of love and understanding, sealed the reconciliation, a testament to their evolving relationship.

Noah's own family journey was equally transformative. His parents, initially apprehensive about his artistic aspirations, had seen the transformation in their son, the newfound confidence, the unwavering determination. They had witnessed the positive impact of his friendship with Liam, the support and encouragement they offered each other. They had observed the growing recognition of Noah's talent, the exhibitions, the positive feedback from the art community. Their reservations gradually diminished, replaced by an overwhelming sense of pride in their son's artistic achievements and the depth of his friendships.

One evening, Liam and Noah attended a gallery opening showcasing Noah's latest collection. Liam's parents were there, his mother radiating pride, his father subtly observing with a newfound appreciation for Noah's talent. Noah's parents were there as well, their eyes shining with love and admiration. They were not just observing their son's work, they were witnessing the profound impact of his art on his life, and on the lives of those around him.

The two families mingled throughout the evening, forging connections beyond their children's friendship. They shared stories, laughter, and meaningful conversations. The initial awkwardness, the hesitant glances, gave way to genuine warmth and acceptance. Liam's mother engaged Noah's mother in a conversation about their sons' artistic aspirations, finding common ground in their shared support and pride. Liam's father quietly complimented one of Noah's paintings, his appreciation evident in his tone. It was a powerful display of unity, a celebration of their sons' friendship, their talent, and their shared journey.

The summer that followed was filled with collaborative projects, family gatherings, and quiet moments of shared joy. Liam and Noah spent their days working on a community mural, their collaborative efforts a reflection of their unique friendship and their shared passion for art. The mural, a vibrant tapestry of color and creativity, became a symbol of their bond, their resilience, and their shared journey.

The families, once separated by unspoken reservations and differing expectations, found common ground in their shared love and admiration for their sons. They celebrated their achievements, offered support during setbacks, and shared life's everyday joys. Family dinners were no longer tense affairs, but rather opportunities for genuine connection, shared laughter, and a growing sense of unity. They had overcome the initial barriers of misunderstanding, forging a new kind of family bond that embraced diversity, cherished individuality, and valued the profound impact of friendship.

This evolved understanding wasn't just about accepting Liam and Noah's relationship; it was about recognizing the intrinsic value of individual passions, the power of genuine friendships, and the transformative potential of empathy and open communication. The families learned that love doesn't always adhere to predetermined expectations; sometimes, the most beautiful connections emerge from defying convention and embracing authenticity. The journey of acceptance was not always easy, but it was a testament to the enduring power of love, understanding, and the unwavering strength of true friendship. It was a powerful narrative of growth, demonstrating how understanding can bridge divides, heal wounds, and create a tapestry of interconnectedness.

Their families became a source of support and encouragement, recognizing the strength and resilience within their sons, a resilience honed by the challenges they had faced and the triumphs they had celebrated together. The summer before college marked not just an end to a chapter, but a beginning of a new narrative, a narrative where family, friendship, and individual passions converged, creating a powerful symphony of love, acceptance, and unwavering support. The quiet moments shared between families became a testament to the transformative power of love, understanding, and a shared journey. Liam and

Noah, their families united, embarked on their individual journeys towards college, carrying with them their dreams and the unwavering support of a family extended by love, respect, and the unique bond of friendship.

The initial awkwardness surrounding Liam and Noah's relationship didn't vanish overnight. It was a slow, subtle shift, like the gradual melting of ice in the spring sun. At first, whispers followed them down the school hallways. Sidelong glances were exchanged, hushed conversations punctuated by nervous giggles. Some classmates maintained a polite distance, offering carefully measured smiles that didn't quite reach their eyes. The usual boisterous camaraderie that characterized their friend group felt...different. A palpable tension hung in the air, an unspoken question mark hovering over their interactions.

The first real test came during the annual school bonfire. The flames crackled and danced, casting flickering shadows on the faces of the students gathered around. The air thrummed with the energy of youthful exuberance, yet Liam and Noah found themselves on the periphery, a silent observer of the energetic hubbub. Their usual ease and confidence seemed to waver, replaced by a hesitant uncertainty. They exchanged a nervous glance, a quiet acknowledgment of the subtle shift in the dynamics of their social circle.

Sarah, one of their closest friends, approached them cautiously. She was always the mediator, the voice of reason, the glue that held their group together. She sat down beside them, her expression thoughtful. "It's...different this year, isn't it?" she murmured, her voice barely above a whisper.

Liam nodded slowly, his gaze fixed on the dancing flames. "Yeah," he agreed, his voice laced with a hint of melancholy. "It feels like...we're on the outside looking in."

Noah, ever the optimist, offered a reassuring smile. "It's just a matter of time," he said, his voice firm. "People will come around. They just need...time."

Sarah's words, however, were more pragmatic. "It's not just time, Noah. It's about understanding. And that takes more than just time. It takes effort." She paused, gathering her thoughts. "Maybe we need to bridge the gap. We need to show everyone that nothing's really changed."

Their conversation sparked a plan. They decided to actively invite their classmates to join them in their usual activities_their regular game nights, the occasional movie marathon, or the trips to the local art gallery. They made a conscious effort to include everyone, to make sure no one felt left out. It wasn't always easy. Some initial hesitancy remained, some awkward silences still punctuated their conversations. But gradually, slowly, the atmosphere shifted.

The turning point came unexpectedly during the school's annual talent show. Noah, ever the confident artist, showcased his latest sculpture, a breathtaking piece that captivated the audience. Despite his usual stage fright, Liam presented a collaborative piece he and Noah had created, a dynamic visual presentation accompanied by Liam's evocative spoken word poetry. Their performance transcended the art itself; it was a testament to their shared passion, deep connection and unwavering support for each other.

The applause was deafening. But more significant than the thunderous applause were the heartfelt smiles, the genuine expressions of admiration on the faces of their classmates. The whispers were gone, replaced by murmurs of appreciation and respect. The hesitant smiles of the previous months had transformed into genuine expressions of warmth and acceptance.

After the show, their classmates surrounded them, congratulating them, their previous reservations replaced by genuine enthusiasm. Mark, who had previously been hesitant, confessed that he'd been wrong to judge. "That was amazing, guys," he said, a genuine smile lighting up his face. "I'm so glad I got to see it." His confession broke down a barrier. Others followed suit, offering their sincere apologies for any past judgment or misunderstanding.

The shift wasn't immediate or complete. There were still moments of awkwardness and occasional sidelong glances. But the overall atmosphere had changed. Their friend group was no longer fractured. It was whole, inclusive, and accepting.

The change extended beyond their immediate social circle. Their teachers observed the shift, noticing the increased camaraderie and inclusivity within the class. At a school assembly, the principal commended Liam and Noah for their bravery, talent and positive influence on their peers. Their story became a quiet example of how open communication and genuine understanding could transcend prejudice and foster acceptance.

The summer following their junior year was filled with a renewed sense of community and shared experiences. They participated in more collaborative projects, their artistic skills complementing each other's strengths. They worked on a large-scale mural for the community center, their artwork a vibrant reflection of the diversity and inclusiveness of their town.

Their families, too, were deeply involved. Liam's father, who had initially been resistant to Liam's art aspirations, became a strong supporter, often visiting the mural site, offering encouragement and lending a hand with the logistics. Noah's mother, who had embraced their relationship from the beginning, helped organize a fundraiser to support the project. The families' participation was a symbol of the broader acceptance that had blossomed within the community.

The impact extended beyond the immediate circle of their families and friends. News of their collaborative efforts spread, attracting attention from local media. An article in the local newspaper highlighted their journey of acceptance, their artistic talent and their positive influence on their community. The article sparked conversations across the town, raising awareness about inclusivity and the importance of celebrating diversity.

This positive shift didn't erase years of societal prejudice but created a ripple effect, a gradually widening circle of acceptance and understanding. Liam and Noah became positive role models within their school and community, proving that authenticity, talent, and genuine connection could transcend societal norms and forge pathways toward a more inclusive and understanding world. Their journey served as a reminder that it's not enough to simply tolerate differences; embracing them, celebrating them, and learning from them is crucial. Their story became a powerful narrative of how acceptance could blossom from understanding and how empathy could bridge the divides that separate individuals and communities. The process wasn't always easy; it required patience, perseverance, and a willingness to engage in open and honest conversations. But the eventual outcome was a testament to the enduring power of human connection and the transformative effect of love and understanding. It was a journey of transformation, not just for Liam and Noah, but for their entire community. And the summer before their senior year became a beacon of hope, showcasing the transformative power of inclusivity and the profound impact of embracing differences.

The summer stretched out before them, a canvas of endless possibilities. The whirlwind of the school year, with its anxieties and triumphs, had finally subsided, leaving behind a quiet calm. For Liam and Noah, this quietude was a fertile ground for introspection, a space to nurture the blossoming confidence that had taken root within them. The public acceptance they'd gained wasn't merely a social victory but a catalyst for a deeper, more profound self-acceptance.

Liam, who had always struggled with self-doubt, found himself revisiting old journals filled with self-deprecating entries and anxieties about his artistic aspirations. He reread them not with shame, but with a newfound perspective. The awkward teenager who worried about his perceived inadequacies was still a part of him, but those insecurities no longer defined him. He saw the evolution of his self-image, the slow but steady growth from hesitant self-consciousness to a burgeoning self-assurance. He'd found a voice, both literally through his poetry and figuratively through his embrace of his identity. This summer was dedicated to exploring that voice fully.

One evening, sitting on his porch swing, the setting sun painting the sky in hues of orange and purple, Liam reread his most recent poem, a piece inspired by his relationship with Noah. He'd never dared to share his more vulnerable poetry before, fearing judgment and ridicule. But now, as he read the words aloud, he felt a surge of pride, not just in his craft, but in his courage to express his truth. He wasn't just writing about his feelings; he was accepting them, embracing them as an integral part of his identity. His self-acceptance wasn't merely a passive acknowledgment but an active, continuous process of self-discovery.

Noah, on the other hand, had always possessed a greater degree of self-confidence, but even he experienced a deepening of his self-awareness. He'd always been open and expressive, but now, he understood the importance of self-care and self-love. He recognized that his strength wasn't merely about his artistic talent or his ability to support Liam, but about his inherent self-worth, independent of external validation.

One day, while they were working on their community mural, a particularly challenging section frustrated Noah. He was meticulous, striving for perfection, and the imperfections in his brushstrokes gnawed at his usually unwavering confidence. Liam, noticing his friend's agitation, gently placed a hand on his shoulder.

"Hey," Liam said softly, his voice laced with understanding, "It's okay. It doesn't have to be perfect. What matters is that we're doing this together, and we're making something beautiful, even if it's not perfect."

Noah looked at Liam, his friend's words resonating deeply. Liam's acceptance of imperfections, both in the artwork and in themselves, was a profound lesson. He realized that his self-worth wasn't contingent on flawless execution. He breathed deeply and, with a newfound lightness, resumed his work. The imperfection he'd been so critical of suddenly felt less significant, a testament to the human touch that imbued the mural with life and authenticity.

Their newfound self-acceptance wasn't solely an individual journey; it was intrinsically linked to their relationship. Their love for each other became a bedrock of support, a safe space where they could explore their vulnerabilities without fear of judgment. They spent countless hours talking, sharing their anxieties and dreams, supporting each other through challenges, and celebrating each other's successes.

Their conversations weren't just about their relationship; they delved into deeper aspects of their individual identities, their aspirations, and their fears.

One evening, nestled under a blanket of stars, they talked about their families. Liam shared his father's growing acceptance, the subtle shifts in his demeanor, the encouraging words that had replaced the initial reservations. Noah recounted his mother's unwavering support, her constant reminders that their love was a testament to their strength and courage. These conversations weren't just about their parents' approval, but about the affirmation of their own self-worth, the realization that their families' acceptance stemmed from their own embracing of their identities. Their relationship had become a catalyst for both their individual and collective self-acceptance.

The public display of their affection, once a source of anxiety, became a testament to their confidence and pride. They held hands without hesitation, sharing a tender embrace in the school hallways or laughing freely in front of their friends. They weren't just claiming their relationship; they were claiming their identities.

Their self-acceptance wasn't a sudden transformation but a gradual process marked by small victories, moments of quiet reflection, and the unwavering support of each other. It involved confronting internalized prejudices, acknowledging past insecurities, and celebrating the beauty of their unique identities. It wasn't about conforming to societal expectations but about embracing their own truth. Their journey wasn't merely about overcoming external obstacles; it was about building a foundation of self-love, a solid base from which they could confidently face the world together. The summer wasn't just a season; it was a period of profound personal growth and self-discovery that blossomed into a vibrant expression of self-acceptance. It was the summer they truly found themselves, as individuals and as a couple, their love a testament to the transformative power of self-acceptance and mutual respect. They stood hand in hand, not just as a couple but as fully realized individuals, ready to face whatever challenges the future held, fortified by their unwavering self-love and unshakeable mutual support.

Their self-acceptance extended beyond their personal lives, influencing their art and their interactions with the community. The mural they created wasn't just a visual masterpiece; it was a reflection of their journey, a vibrant testament to their self-acceptance and the inclusive spirit they had fostered within their community. The colors, the imagery, and even the paint's texture spoke of their personal growth and their journey from insecurity to self-assuredness. The mural itself became a symbol of their transformation, a public declaration of their identity and their commitment to inclusivity.

As the summer drew close, Liam and Noah felt a profound sense of peace and fulfillment. The challenges they had faced, the struggles they had overcome, had strengthened their bond, deepening their understanding of themselves and each other. Their journey was far from over, but they were equipped with the self-acceptance and resilience necessary to navigate whatever the future might bring. The path to self-acceptance was a continuous journey, but they knew, hand in hand, they would continue to traverse it together, supporting and empowering each other every step of the way. Their story wasn't just about finding love; it was about finding themselves, embracing their identities, and celebrating the beauty of their unique selves, together.

The late summer sun cast long shadows across the town square as Liam and Noah worked on their final touches for the community mural. Liam, ever the poet, focused on the delicate details, adding subtle nuances of color and texture that breathed life into the scene. His artistic expression was a whisper, a soft caress of paint that evoked emotion rather than a bold statement. Noah, on the other hand, attacked his section with a vibrant energy, his brushstrokes bold and decisive. He filled the canvas with a riot of color and movement, his style a stark contrast to Liam's quieter approach. Yet, there was a harmony in their differences, a balance that reflected the essence of their relationship.

They didn't try to conform to each other's styles; instead, they embraced the contrast, recognizing that the beauty of the mural lay in its diversity. Liam's sections were contemplative and introspective, while Noah's bursts were energetic and expressive. Where Liam's brushstrokes were gentle and flowing,

Noah's were sharp and defined. The juxtaposition wasn't jarring; it was complementary, a testament to the unique strength of their individual talents.

They'd learned that their differences weren't weaknesses but rather sources of strength. Liam's introspective nature balanced Noah's extroverted energy, and Noah's confidence often helped him push past his self-doubt. They'd become a harmonious blend of opposing forces, a testament to the beauty of unity within diversity. Their collaboration on the mural was more than just an artistic endeavor; it was a reflection of their relationship, a vibrant tapestry woven from the threads of their individual experiences and perspectives.

One afternoon, as they worked side-by-side, a group of younger children approached them, their eyes wide with wonder. They asked Liam and Noah questions about their art, their voices filled with innocent curiosity. Liam patiently answered their questions, explaining his artistic process with a gentle calmness. Noah, ever the charismatic one, captivated them with stories about the mural's inspiration, his words filled with infectious enthusiasm. The children were fascinated by the differences in their approaches, their questions revealing a natural curiosity about the unique personalities of the artists.

Later that evening, as they sat together, the vibrant colors of the sunset mirrored the vibrant colors of their completed mural; Liam reflected on this interaction. "It's amazing, isn't it?" he said, his voice soft with wonder. "How those kids could see the beauty in both our styles, even though they're so different."

Noah nodded, his eyes twinkling. "It's because they haven't yet learned to judge," he said. "They see the art, they see the beauty, they don't see the need for it to fit into some pre-conceived mold."

Liam's insight deepened further. "Maybe that's what we need to remember, too," he mused. "To see the beauty in differences, to appreciate the unique qualities that each person brings to the table."

Their conversations extended beyond art, delving into other aspects of their lives. They discussed their respective families, the ongoing evolution of their relationships with their parents, and the ever-increasing acceptance they received. Liam's father, initially hesitant, now openly expressed pride in his son's artistry and his relationship with Noah. He even volunteered to help with the community garden project that Noah spearheaded, an unexpected gesture that spoke volumes about his evolving acceptance.

Noah's mother, ever the supportive force, continued to be their unwavering champion. She organized a small gathering to celebrate the mural's completion, inviting friends, family, and community members. The event became a testament to their journey, a gathering that celebrated their art, resilience, love, and embrace of diversity. The food represented the cultural diversity of their town, a reflection of their commitment to inclusivity. The music was a mix of genres, ranging from soulful blues to energetic pop, mirroring the eclectic nature of their own personalities.

Through shared activities, their individual strengths and talents blossomed. Liam, inspired by their shared experiences, started a poetry workshop for teenagers, using his art as a tool to promote self-expression and self-acceptance. Using his organizational skills and charisma, Noah established a youth mentorship program, connecting young adults with inspiring figures from diverse backgrounds. Their contributions extended far beyond their immediate circle, impacting the broader community profoundly.

They organized a community potluck, bringing together people from all walks of life, sharing stories and laughter, celebrating their differences rather than allowing them to create divisions. They learned to appreciate the distinct perspectives of others, understanding that their unique qualities enriched their shared experiences. They learned the importance of active listening, of valuing the input of others, of appreciating the perspectives that differed from their own.

They even collaborated on a series of short films, Liam writing the scripts and Noah handling the cinematography. Their combined talents resulted in a collection of visually stunning and emotionally resonant short films that explored themes of self-discovery, identity, and resilience. These films became a local sensation, winning awards at various film festivals and generating positive feedback from the community.

This wasn't just about individual success but the strength of their collaboration and the power of their shared vision. Their differences didn't hinder them; they enhanced their creativity and broadened their artistic reach. The films showcased not only their individual talents but the harmonious blend of their contrasting styles, a testament to the beauty of their shared journey.

As the summer drew close, Liam and Noah stood before their completed mural, a masterpiece that reflected their journey of self-discovery and mutual acceptance. It was a vibrant tapestry woven with threads of their individual experiences, a testament to the beauty of diversity and the power of embracing differences. The mural was more than just painted on a wall; it was a reflection of their growth, their resilience, and their love for each other and their community. It was a beacon of hope, a symbol of unity in diversity, a testament to the transformative power of acceptance and understanding. Their journey was far from over, but they stood ready to face the future; their bond strengthened by their unwavering commitment to embracing their differences and celebrating the unique qualities of themselves and others. Their love story was a testament to the power of self-acceptance and mutual respect, a reminder that our differences are not weaknesses but rather sources of strength, enriching our lives and fostering a deeper understanding of ourselves and the world around us.

The crisp autumn air carried the scent of woodsmoke and fallen leaves as Liam and Noah sat on their porch, warming their hands with a steaming mug of hot chocolate. The mural, a vibrant testament to their summer's work, stood proudly in the town square, a constant reminder of their shared journey. But now, as the leaves changed color and the days grew shorter, their focus shifted from the past to the future.

Liam, his gaze lost in the swirling patterns of the clouds, spoke softly, "I've been thinking... about the poetry workshop." He traced a pattern on his mug with a finger, a thoughtful frown creasing his brow. "It's been incredibly rewarding, connecting with those teenagers, seeing them find their voices through poetry. But I want to do more. I want to expand it, maybe offer workshops in different schools, even create a small publishing imprint for their work."

Noah, ever practical, leaned forward, his eyes bright with enthusiasm. "That's amazing, Liam! I can help with the logistics, find sponsorships, maybe even design a website to showcase their work. We could even create a yearly anthology featuring the best poems from the workshops." He paused, a playful grin spreading across his face. "Think of it - 'Emerging Voices: A Liam and Noah Project.'"

The idea sparked a flurry of excited conversation. They brainstormed potential sponsors, discussed curriculum development, and even sketched out possible website designs. Liam's artistic vision combined seamlessly with Noah's organizational prowess, their complementary skills creating a synergy that fueled their enthusiasm. They realized that their individual talents weren't just personal strengths; they were tools that could positively impact their community, allowing them to share their passion and inspire others.

The conversation then drifted to Noah's mentorship program. He spoke passionately about the young adults he'd connected with, the diverse backgrounds they represented, and the unique challenges they faced. He spoke of a young woman aspiring to become a doctor, a young man struggling to find his footing after a difficult family situation, and a group of teenagers keen to learn more about sustainable agriculture. Each story was a testament to the power of human connection and the importance of providing guidance and support.

Liam listened intently, offering insightful suggestions. He suggested the use of storytelling and creative writing exercises to help the mentees process their experiences and discover their strengths. He offered to write short motivational pieces for their online platform, adding a creative touch to their guidance. This mutual support, built on their deep understanding of each other, transformed their individual projects into a collaborative endeavor, enhancing their impact and deepening their connection.

Their discussions extended far beyond their individual projects, reaching into the realm of their shared future. They talked about the possibility of buying a small house together, maybe in a quiet neighborhood with a garden. Liam envisioned a cozy space filled with books, paintings, and the aroma of brewing tea. Noah pictured a sprawling garden overflowing with herbs and vegetables, a testament to their shared commitment to sustainable living.

The conversations weren't always grand plans and ambitious projects. There were moments of quiet contemplation, too, moments of shared silence as they watched the sunset, the fiery hues mirroring the warmth in their hearts. These moments of peaceful reflection were as crucial as their enthusiastic planning sessions. They provided an opportunity to acknowledge the journey they'd taken, the challenges overcome, and the strength of their bond.

One evening, as they sat curled up on the sofa, Liam gently picked up a framed photograph of the completed mural. "Remember when we started this?" he asked, his voice soft with nostalgia. "I was so nervous, so unsure of myself."

Noah smiled, reaching out to take Liam's hand. "And look at us now," he said, his voice filled with pride and love. "We've created something beautiful together. And we're only just getting started."

Their journey, they realized, wasn't just about achieving individual goals; it was about building a life together, a life filled with mutual respect, shared ambitions, and unwavering support. They understood that their individual strengths were complementary, their differences enriching their lives and deepening their bond. It was a journey of mutual growth, a testament to the power of acceptance, understanding, and unwavering love.

Their future wasn't a pre-defined path, but a canvas waiting to be painted with their shared dreams. They were excited to see what the future held, confident in their ability to face any challenges that came their way, knowing they would face them together, hand in hand, their love a constant source of strength and inspiration.

They started researching sustainable building materials for their dream house, considering the environmental impact of their choices. Liam sketched designs, incorporating elements of nature into the architecture, while Noah researched eco-friendly building practices and energy-efficient solutions. Their combined knowledge and passion resulted in detailed plans for a house that reflected their shared values and aesthetic sensibilities.

They explored different locations, envisioning their future life in various settings. They discussed the pros and cons of living in the city, close to cultural activities and career opportunities, versus living in the countryside, surrounded by nature and tranquility. They knew the decision wasn't just about a location; it was about finding a place to nurture their growth and support their shared vision of a life filled with love, creativity, and meaningful work.

One evening, while attending a community event, they met an architect specializing in sustainable building. They discussed their project, and the architect was impressed by their detailed plans and commitment to environmental responsibility. This encounter led to a professional collaboration, further solidifying their plans and providing them with expert guidance.

Liam started experimenting with new artistic techniques, inspired by his ongoing work with teenagers in the poetry workshops. He discovered a newfound passion for digital art, expanding his creative expression beyond traditional mediums. Noah, meanwhile, utilized his organizational skills to create a comprehensive fundraising plan for their future home, combining online crowdfunding with personal donations from their extended network.

Their journey was a continuous process of learning, growth, and mutual support. They supported each other's personal and professional pursuits, celebrating each other's successes and offering comfort during moments of self-doubt. They knew that their success wasn't just about individual achievements but about their shared journey, their bond strengthened by their unwavering commitment to one another.

As the winter approached, they finalized the plans for their dream house, a space that would reflect their unique personalities and shared vision for the future. They selected a quiet neighborhood on the outskirts of town, a peaceful setting nestled amongst rolling hills and whispering trees. The design incorporated natural light, sustainable materials, and elements that connected them to the surrounding environment. It was a house that felt like home, a sanctuary where they could nurture their creativity, pursue their ambitions, and build a life filled with love, laughter and shared dreams. Their future wasn't just a destination; it was a journey they were embarking on together, their love story a testament to the transformative power of acceptance, understanding, and shared aspirations. Their journey had just begun, and they were ready for whatever the future held… together.

Chapter 4
Highs and Lows

The initial euphoria of their shared successes began to subtly shift as the reality of their ambitious plans settled in. The first crack appeared during a particularly intense brainstorming session for the poetry anthology. Fueled by artistic passion, Liam envisioned a visually stunning, almost avant-garde design replete with unconventional typography and abstract imagery. Noah, ever the pragmatist, countered with a more streamlined, user-friendly design, emphasizing clear navigation and easy accessibility for a wider audience. The disagreement, initially a playful exchange of ideas, escalated into a heated debate. Liam felt his creative vision was being compromised, his artistic integrity questioned. Noah, in turn, felt his concerns about practicality and accessibility were being dismissed. The air crackled with unspoken frustrations, the comfortable rhythm of their collaboration momentarily disrupted.

Their usual easy communication faltered. Liam retreated into a quiet sulk, sketching furiously in his notebook, his brow furrowed in concentration or perhaps, frustration. Sensing the distance, Noah attempted to bridge the gap, offering compromises and suggestions, but his attempts were met with short, clipped responses. The silence that followed felt heavier than any argument, a stark contrast to their usual vibrant interactions. The comfortable familiarity of their relationship seemed to fray at the edges, a subtle but unsettling shift in their dynamic.

The tension didn't just reside in their professional collaborations. It seeped into their personal lives, subtly coloring their evening conversations and shared moments. The usual easy laughter felt forced, replaced by strained silences and averted gazes. Even the shared joy of planning their dream house, once a source of immense excitement, became a source of simmering friction. Liam's preference for a minimalist design clashed with Noah's desire for a more rustic, traditional aesthetic. Arguments flared about the choice of flooring, the placement of windows, even the color of the paint. The dream house, once a symbol of their shared future, now seemed to represent their growing chasm.

One particularly tense evening, amidst a heated discussion about the placement of a garden shed, Liam blurted out, "It feels like you're always trying to control things, Noah. My ideas, my vision... everything." The words hung in the air, raw and accusatory. Noah recoiled, his eyes wide with hurt. "That's not fair, Liam. I'm just trying to be practical. We need to consider the budget, the feasibility..." His voice trailed off, the weight of his unspoken anxieties surfacing. The argument escalated and a torrent of pent-up frustrations unleashed. They accused each other of selfishness, of not listening, of not understanding. The shared dreams that had bound them together now felt like a battlefield.

The aftermath was a painful silence, broken only by the occasional sigh or a nervous clearing of the throat. They both retreated into themselves, replaying the argument in their heads, dissecting their words and intentions. The realization dawned on them both that their comfortable silence hadn't solved anything. It only magnified their differences. They had allowed their differing approaches to overshadow their shared love and mutual respect.

The breakthrough came unexpectedly during a quiet walk in the woods. The crisp autumn air and the rustle of leaves seemed to soothe their frayed nerves. Liam, breaking the silence, apologized for his harsh words, acknowledging his own insecurities and the fear that his artistic vision wasn't being valued. Noah, in turn, apologized for his rigid practicality, admitting that he had failed to appreciate Liam's creative process and the emotional investment he poured into his work.

They spoke openly and honestly, acknowledging their individual needs and fears. They discovered that their conflicts stemmed not from malice or a lack of love but from differing communication styles and unmet emotional needs. Liam needed reassurance and validation for his artistic expression, while Noah required a sense of security and practicality in their joint endeavors. They learned to articulate these needs, to listen empathetically, and to find common ground through compromise and mutual respect.

This newfound understanding permeated all aspects of their lives. In their professional collaborations, they implemented a collaborative decision-making system, ensuring that their artistic vision and practical considerations were equally valued. They agreed to openly discuss their concerns, to actively listen to each other's perspectives, and to seek compromise rather than confrontation. The result was a more balanced and fulfilling approach to their projects, enhancing their impact and strengthening their bond.

The design of their dream house became a testament to their newfound understanding. They integrated both Liam's minimalist aesthetic and Noah's preference for rustic charm, creating a home that reflected their individuality while celebrating their shared vision. The discussions were no longer fraught with tension but filled with collaboration and compromise, resulting in a design that felt genuinely representative of their combined personalities and dreams.

Their journey of conflict resolution wasn't a linear one. There were moments of relapse when old habits resurfaced and disagreements flared. However, their foundation of open communication and mutual understanding proved strong enough to weather these storms. They learned to forgive, to empathize, and to approach disagreements with patience and understanding.

The conflicts, initially painful and disruptive, ultimately strengthened their bond. They discovered the importance of healthy conflict resolution, not as a destructive force, but as an opportunity for growth and deeper intimacy. They realized that the ability to navigate disagreements respectfully was as crucial to their relationship as shared dreams and unwavering love.

Their journey served as a testament to the resilience of their connection, forged not just in moments of shared joy and success, but also in the crucible of conflict and compromise. The house, now under construction, stood as a physical manifestation of their growth, a home built not just on bricks and mortar, but on a foundation of mutual understanding, forgiveness, and unwavering love. The challenges they faced weren't just overcome; they served as stepping stones towards a stronger, more profound connection, a testament to the enduring power of their love story.

The following weeks were a delicate dance of tiptoeing around unspoken anxieties. The vibrant energy that had once characterized their interactions was replaced by cautious politeness, a fragile truce rather than genuine reconciliation. While the overt arguments had ceased, a subtle undercurrent of tension persisted, a lingering echo of their past conflicts. Liam found himself hyper-aware of Noah's reactions, second-guessing his every word and action. He'd catch Noah staring intently, a mixture of concern and guardedness in his eyes, and the familiar knot of apprehension would tighten in his stomach.

One evening, while sorting through the mountain of paperwork related to the poetry anthology, Liam stumbled upon a draft of a design proposal that Noah had apparently discarded. It was strikingly similar to Liam's original concept, albeit simplified and more commercially viable. A wave of frustration washed over Liam. It felt as though Noah had subtly appropriated his ideas, albeit with a layer of "practicality" that diluted the artistic integrity he'd fiercely guarded.

He confronted Noah that night, his voice tight with suppressed anger. The argument that ensued wasn't a screaming match, but a slow burn of accusations and hurt feelings. Liam felt betrayed, his trust violated. He expressed his pain, not just over the design, but over a perceived pattern of Noah subtly undermining his artistic vision.

Noah, visibly shaken, vehemently denied any intentional appropriation, explaining that he had simply been trying to synthesize their ideas, finding a balance between Liam's artistic passion and market demands. He confessed to his insecurity about Liam's sometimes-unconventional ideas, his fear that they wouldn't appeal to a wider audience, leading him to try and bridge the gap on his own. He apologized for not communicating his concerns directly and for taking a shortcut instead of having an open and honest conversation.

This conversation, though painful, proved to be a turning point. It wasn't a single, sweeping resolution, but a beginning. It forced them to confront the deeper issues underlying their conflicts - the fear of vulnerability, the unspoken anxieties, the need for validation. They began attending couples counseling, a decision initially met with hesitation but ultimately proved invaluable.

The therapist helped them unpack their communication styles, illuminating the subtle ways in which their differences were fueling their conflicts. Liam, it turned out, expressed his needs indirectly, often relying on passive-aggressive behavior to communicate his frustration. On the other hand, Noah favored direct communication but often lacked the emotional intelligence to deliver his concerns without sounding critical or dismissive. Through guided exercises and open discussions, they began to understand each other's emotional language and develop healthier communication strategies.

One of the most significant breakthroughs came when they discussed the concept of trust. Liam expressed his fear that Noah didn't truly value his artistic vision, that his practicality always overshadowed his creativity. Noah, in turn, confessed to his own anxieties, his fear of financial instability, his concern about the long-term viability of their creative endeavors. They realized that their insecurities were feeding into their conflicts, distorting their perceptions and hindering their ability to communicate openly and honestly. They acknowledged the importance of vulnerability, of openly sharing their fears and insecurities without fear of judgment.

The therapist introduced them to the concept of "active listening," a skill that proved transformative. They learned to listen not just to hear the words, but to understand the underlying emotions and intentions. They practiced paraphrasing each other's statements, ensuring that they understood each other's perspectives before responding. This simple yet powerful technique drastically reduced misunderstandings and paved the way for more constructive conversations.

Their commitment to honesty extended beyond their personal struggles. They became more transparent in their professional collaborations, openly sharing their anxieties, doubts, and creative frustrations. They established a system of regular check-ins, allowing them to address concerns promptly and prevent minor disagreements from escalating into major conflicts. They learned to value each other's differing perspectives, recognizing that their contrasting approaches often complemented each other, resulting in a richer and more nuanced output.

The process was far from easy. There were setbacks, moments of frustration, and the occasional relapse into old patterns of communication. But their commitment to honesty and trust served as a bedrock, a constant reminder that open and honest communication, even amidst disagreements, was essential for maintaining a healthy relationship. They learned to approach conflicts not as personal attacks but as opportunities for growth and mutual understanding. They discovered that the ability to navigate disagreements with grace and empathy strengthened their bond, creating a deeper level of intimacy and mutual respect.

As their relationship deepened, their communication evolved. They learned to embrace vulnerability, to share their deepest fears and insecurities without reservation. This vulnerability fostered a level of trust that transcended the challenges they had faced. They began to appreciate the complexities of their individual personalities, their contrasting strengths and weaknesses. They realized that their differences were not a source of division but a testament to the richness and diversity of their relationship. The shared successes continued to flow, but now they were fueled by a deeper understanding, a foundation of unwavering trust and honest communication.

The design of their dream house became a symbol of their journey. The initial disagreements about aesthetic preferences had nearly shattered their relationship, but now, their combined vision reflected a harmonious blend of their individual tastes, a testament to their ability to navigate differences and find common ground. The house, when finally completed, wasn't merely a structure of bricks and mortar, but a living testament to their shared growth, a reflection of their enduring commitment to honesty, trust, and open communication.

Their journey of growth and reconciliation wasn't linear; it was a winding path filled with challenges, setbacks, and moments of profound self-discovery. Yet, through it all, their commitment to honest communication remained unwavering. They learned that vulnerability wasn't a weakness but a strength, a courageous act of self-expression that deepened their connection. They discovered that true intimacy stemmed not from the absence of conflict but from the willingness to confront disagreements with openness, empathy, and a shared commitment to understanding. The foundation of their relationship, built on trust and honesty, stood strong, a beacon of resilience amidst the inevitable storms of life. Their story became a testament to the transformative power of open communication, a reminder that even the most challenging conflicts can pave the way for a deeper, more profound connection. The house, finally standing complete, wasn't just a symbol of their success, but a living representation of their growth, a testament to a love story forged in the crucible of honesty and unwavering trust.

Liam's grandmother, Nana Rose, the woman who had filled his childhood with stories and laughter, was diagnosed with a rapidly progressing form of dementia. The news hit him like a physical blow, leaving him reeling with a grief that felt both immediate and anticipatory. He found himself oscillating between anger at the unfairness of it all and a desperate, clinging need to hold onto the woman who had been his anchor. He spent hours by her bedside, reading aloud from her favorite books, trying to reach her through the fog that was gradually obscuring her mind.

He didn't know how to process his emotions. The vibrant energy that had characterized his interactions with Noah was muted; he wasn't sure what to say or how to say it. He felt like a ship lost at sea, tossed about by waves of grief and helplessness. He tried to maintain a façade of normalcy, but the weight of his sorrow was palpable.

Noah, sensing Liam's distress, was his constant rock. He didn't offer platitudes or empty reassurances. Instead, he simply *was* there; a quiet, steady presence, holding Liam's hand, offering a shoulder to cry on, making sure Liam ate, slept, and didn't completely unravel. He helped arrange Nana Rose's care, handled the endless stream of practical details, and shielded Liam from the burden of managing the logistics. He absorbed the frustration Liam didn't know how to articulate, offering unwavering support without judgement.

One evening, Liam broke down completely, the suppressed grief overwhelming him. He wept uncontrollably, the raw, ragged sobs tearing at his insides. Noah simply held him, stroking his hair, whispering words of comfort that felt more like a balm on a wound than empty words. He didn't try to fix anything. He just held the space for Liam's pain, allowing him to experience it without judgment or expectation.

"I don't know what to do," Liam choked out between sobs. "I feel so... lost."

Noah tightened his hold, his embrace a silent promise of steadfastness. "You're not alone," he murmured. "We'll get through this together."

Beyond the immediate crisis, Noah's support extended to the long, slow decline. He accompanied Liam to every doctor's appointment, patiently taking notes, asking questions and advocating for Nana Rose's best care. He even learned how to use the specialized equipment to support Nana Rose's comfort. He understood that Liam needed to be present for Nana Rose, and he facilitated that, shouldering the burden of everyday life so that Liam could focus on spending quality time with his grandmother.

Meanwhile, Noah's own world was facing upheaval. His father, a man who had always been distant and emotionally unavailable, had suffered a heart attack. The experience forced Noah to confront unresolved issues from his past, issues he hadn't previously shared with Liam. He found himself struggling with the complex mixture of guilt, fear, and unexpected tenderness that emerged from this unexpected crisis.

The news of Noah's father's illness cast a long shadow over their shared time with Nana Rose. However, this crisis brought a different kind of strength to their already-strengthened bond. Liam was suddenly aware that Noah held anxieties and fears that he had never verbalized. This newfound understanding allowed Liam to not only provide comfort but also acknowledge and appreciate the struggles Noah was undergoing silently.

Liam, drawing from the strength Noah had offered him during his own crisis, offered unwavering support. He listened patiently as Noah unburdened himself, sharing the complex emotions churning within him. He understood the weight of family expectations, the burden of unspoken resentments, and the struggle to reconcile his desire for a close relationship with his father with the reality of their strained connection. He reminded Noah of his own resilience and the inherent strength that had carried them both through previous storms.

They supported each other through hospital visits, phone calls, and quiet evenings spent simply holding each other. Liam helped Noah navigate the logistical challenges of caring for his father from afar, offering practical assistance and emotional support. He understood the burden that Noah was carrying and offered a space for him to unpack his emotions.

The parallel struggles brought them even closer. They understood each other's vulnerabilities in a way they hadn't before.

They found a shared understanding of the messy, complicated emotions that accompany family illness. They learned to navigate grief and uncertainty together, their love becoming a source of strength and comfort in the face of adversity. They discovered a newfound appreciation for the importance of family, not just the families they were born into, but the family they had built together.

Through the shared experience, their love deepened, their commitment strengthened. The challenges they faced brought them closer, forging a bond that was stronger and more resilient than ever before. They had faced adversity before, but the depth of their mutual support during these two separate yet equally challenging periods solidified their bond, making it unbreakable. They learned the true meaning of love, not as the absence of conflict, but as the unwavering presence of support in the face of life's inevitable storms. The shared experiences revealed a depth of understanding and empathy that enriched their relationship in ways they had never anticipated. They realized that their love story wasn't just about romantic moments, but about facing life's challenges with resilience, compassion, and unwavering support for one another. Their journey had taken unexpected turns, but the constant thread that held them together was the strength of their bond, the understanding they found in shared vulnerabilities and the unwavering support they offered each other during their most difficult times. They had navigated stormy seas and emerged stronger, their relationship a testament to the power of unconditional love and the unwavering strength found in mutual support. The house they had built together, now more than just a structure of bricks and mortar, stood as a symbol of their shared journey, a testament to their love and the unshakeable foundation they had built upon the pillars of trust, honesty, and unwavering support. Their love story was far from over, but the chapters they had already written together were filled with the raw, honest emotion of a love that had weathered the storms and emerged more beautiful than ever. The challenges had not broken them; they had forged them into something stronger, their bond a testament to the enduring power of love, support, and unwavering commitment.

The weeks that followed were a blur of hospital visits, hushed phone calls, and stolen moments of quiet intimacy amidst the chaos. Liam, having witnessed Noah's quiet strength during his own ordeal, now found himself in the role of supporting Noah. He listened patiently as Noah recounted the strained relationship with his father, a man who had always been emotionally distant, a man who had rarely offered a kind word or a comforting hug. The heart attack had, paradoxically, cracked open something within Noah's father, a fragile vulnerability that both terrified and intrigued him.

Noah's father, initially resistant to any sort of emotional engagement, began to slowly thaw. He started to offer halting apologies for his past failings, for the emotional distance he'd maintained. These apologies weren't grand pronouncements; they were whispered regrets, mumbled between breaths, choked with emotion. Noah listened, not necessarily forgiving immediately but allowing himself to hear the words, to understand the regret behind them.

There were still moments of friction, of course. Old patterns of behavior were difficult to break, years of emotional neglect were not easily erased. Noah's father's attempts at connection felt awkward, hesitant, tinged with the uncertainty of a man unaccustomed to expressing his emotions. Yet, in these fumbling attempts, a glimmer of hope emerged. Noah, in turn, found himself softening, his heart opening to the possibility of a genuine relationship with his father.

One evening, after a particularly tense visit to the hospital, Noah and Liam found themselves sitting on the porch swing, the quiet hum of crickets filling the night air. The unspoken weight of recent events hung between them, a palpable tension that needed to be addressed.

"I... I messed up," Noah began, his voice barely a whisper. He was referring not just to a specific event but to a pattern of behavior, a lifetime of suppressing his emotions, of holding himself back from true intimacy. "I haven't been the best partner lately. I've been so focused on my father that I haven't given you the attention you deserve."

Liam reached out and took Noah's hand, his touch gentle and reassuring. "I know," he said softly. "It's okay. I understand. We're both going through a lot."

But Liam had his own unspoken grievances. There had been moments of frustration, of feeling neglected, of silently wishing for more open communication. He had held back, afraid to burden Noah with his own anxieties during such a tumultuous time. The unspoken resentment had begun to build, a silent pressure that threatened to strain their relationship.

This time, Liam decided not to hold back. "But," he continued, his voice gaining strength, "I wish you'd talked to me sooner. About your father, about how you were feeling. Keeping it all inside... it made me feel like I was on the outside looking in."

Noah met Liam's gaze, his eyes filled with remorse. "I'm sorry," he said, his voice thick with emotion. "I know I should have shared more. I was scared. Scared of being a burden, scared of letting you see my vulnerabilities."

Liam squeezed his hand, a silent gesture of understanding. "I'm not going anywhere," he said, his voice firm yet tender. "I want to be there for you, always. But I need you to let me be there. To let me help."

The conversation flowed more easily after that initial outpouring of emotion. They talked, truly talked, about their fears, their anxieties, their unspoken resentments. They acknowledged the pain they had inadvertently caused each other, the misunderstandings that had created distance between them. The process wasn't easy; there were tears, moments of anger, even some raised voices. But within the honesty, within the vulnerability, a healing began.

Liam realized that Noah's emotional suppression wasn't a personal slight, but a manifestation of his own deep-seated insecurities and anxieties, anxieties stemming from his upbringing and his complex relationship with his father. He understood that Noah's hesitancy to share his struggles wasn't a rejection of their connection, but a self-preservation mechanism rooted in his past experiences.

Similarly, Noah came to understand that Liam's desire for more open communication wasn't a criticism of his commitment, but a natural yearning for intimacy and shared vulnerability. He realized that Liam's silent grievances had stemmed from a place of love and concern, a desire to share the burden rather than bear it alone.

The process of forgiveness wasn't a single event, but a gradual unfolding, a slow unwinding of unspoken resentments and misunderstandings. It was about recognizing the human fallibility of each other, the imperfections that made them who they were, the complexities that shaped their responses. It was about empathy, understanding, and a willingness to meet each other's needs, even when they were expressed imperfectly or hesitantly.

As they navigated the complexities of their relationship, they discovered a deeper understanding of themselves and each other. They learned that forgiveness wasn't about erasing the past but integrating it into their present, learning from the mistakes, and building a stronger, more resilient bond. It wasn't about condoning hurtful actions, but about acknowledging the pain, processing the emotions, and moving forward with renewed empathy and compassion.

Forgiveness, they realized, wasn't a sign of weakness but a testament to the strength of their love. It was a conscious choice to prioritize their connection, to nurture their relationship through the inevitable bumps in the road. It was an act of faith, a belief in the potential for growth and healing, even in the face of hurt and disappointment.

The shared experience of caring for their loved ones, of witnessing vulnerability and fragility, had opened their hearts to a deeper level of empathy. They found themselves appreciating the small moments, the shared silences, the quiet gestures of affection that spoke volumes about their commitment. The foundation of their relationship, already strong, now stood on an even firmer ground, strengthened by the shared experience of pain, resilience, and unwavering commitment to one another. Their love story, once characterized by moments of joy and laughter, now included a richer tapestry of understanding, empathy, and the profound strength found in forgiveness and reconciliation.

Their love wasn't merely a romantic ideal; it was a testament to the resilience of the human spirit, the power of human connection, and the transformative capacity of forgiveness. It was a love forged in the fires of adversity, a love that had weathered the storms and emerged stronger, more vibrant, and more deeply rooted than ever before. The house they shared, now more than just a physical structure, stood as a symbol of their enduring love, a testament to their journey of understanding, compassion, and unwavering commitment, a beacon of hope amidst life's inevitable storms. Their story wasn't just about romantic love; it was about the enduring power of human connection, the transformative strength of forgiveness, and the unwavering commitment to a love that could withstand anything life threw their way. Their challenges had not broken them; they had refined them, purified their love, and forged a bond that was as strong and unbreakable as the very foundations of the home they shared. Their future chapters remained unwritten, but they approached them with newfound clarity and confidence, knowing that the love they shared was a force strong enough to weather any storm.

The following weeks saw a gradual shift in their dynamic. The intensity of the crisis had subsided, replaced by a quieter, more settled rhythm. The constant hospital visits lessened, replaced by more frequent phone calls to Noah's father, who continued to navigate this new, unfamiliar territory of emotional expression. Liam, ever observant, noticed the subtle changes; a softer tone in his voice, a slightly less rigid posture, the occasional hesitant smile. Noah, too, was subtly different, more present, more engaged in their everyday life.

One Saturday morning, Liam woke to find Noah already up, brewing coffee and humming softly to himself. He was immersed in a book, a worn copy of poetry he'd mentioned weeks earlier, his brow furrowed in concentration. Liam smiled; this was the Noah he knew and loved - the quiet, introspective soul who found solace in the written word. It starkly contrasted the tense, withdrawn Noah of the past few weeks, and Liam felt a swell of relief. He sat quietly, watching him, letting the moment stretch out, savoring the quiet intimacy. This was balance, he realized... the peaceful coexistence of their individual selves within the larger framework of their relationship.

Later that day, they spent the afternoon exploring a local art fair. Noah, usually more comfortable in quiet spaces, surprised Liam by enthusiastically engaging with the artists, discussing their techniques and inspirations. Liam, a natural extrovert, effortlessly navigated the crowds, chatting with fellow art enthusiasts and securing them some delicious street food. They each reveled in their individual experiences within the shared activity, neither feeling the need to compromise their preferences. The day ended with a picnic in a nearby park, the sun setting in a blaze of glory behind them, painting the sky in shades of orange and purple.

That evening, curled up on the sofa, they watched a movie, Liam's choice - a lighthearted comedy that had him laughing uproariously. Noah, though not usually a fan of slapstick humour, found himself chuckling along, charmed by Liam's contagious laughter and the pure joy it brought. There was a comfortable silence between them, a silent understanding that neither felt the need to fill the void with conversation constantly. Liam mused that this was the beauty of their connection: the ability to share quiet moments without the pressure of forced interaction. It was a testament to the trust and intimacy they had built.

The following week, Liam surprised Noah with tickets to a football game, knowing how much Noah enjoyed the sport. While Liam's interest was more casual, he went along willingly, embracing the crowd's energy and the game's thrill, understanding that this was a small but significant act of love and support for Noah's passion. In return, Noah took Liam to a quiet bookstore, where they spent an afternoon browsing and sharing recommendations. This reciprocal act of embracing each other's passions solidified their understanding of balance in their relationship. It wasn't about sacrificing individual desires for the sake of togetherness; it was about finding a rhythm that accommodated both their distinct preferences.

The balance they found extended beyond hobbies and leisure activities. They established a routine that respected each other's need for alone time. Noah dedicated mornings to his writing, a crucial part of his identity, while Liam focused on his work, finding solace in the early morning hours of uninterrupted focus. Evenings were often shared, but not always; sometimes they dined together and sometimes they chose separate activities, each respecting the other's need for personal space. This wasn't indifference; it was a conscious decision to cultivate individual independence, recognizing that a strong partnership required each individual to remain whole and fulfilled in their own right.

One evening, as they sat on their porch swing, the gentle breeze rustling the leaves of the nearby trees, Noah spoke about his upcoming exhibition. He was anxious, a familiar knot of self-doubt tightening in his stomach. Liam listened patiently, offering words of encouragement and validation. He didn't try to minimize Noah's anxiety, but acknowledged its validity, recognizing it as a natural part of the creative process. He reminded Noah of his talent, his dedication, and his unique voice, reinforcing his belief in Noah's capabilities. He reassured Noah that his worth was not contingent on the success of the exhibition, reminding him that he loved and valued him regardless of external validation.

Liam, in turn, confided in Noah about a challenging project at work. He felt the pressure mounting, the weight of expectations pressing down on him. Noah listened empathetically, offering pragmatic advice and words of comfort. He reminded Liam of his resilience, his ability to handle pressure, and his innate talent for problem-solving. He affirmed Liam's worth, emphasizing his competence and his unique contributions to his profession. The conversation flowed naturally, a testament to their newfound openness and trust. It wasn't about solving each other's problems, but about providing mutual support and understanding, a supportive shoulder to lean on, without diminishing each other's individuality or autonomy.

This reciprocal support became a cornerstone of their relationship. They learned to navigate disagreements with respect and understanding, appreciating that differences of opinion didn't necessarily threaten their bond. They acknowledged each other's emotional needs, recognizing that sometimes silence was just as meaningful as words. They learned to celebrate each other's successes, both big and small, recognizing that each achievement was a testament to their individual strength and perseverance. Their relationship evolved into a partnership that nurtured and empowered both of them, a partnership where individual growth and shared connection thrived side-by-side.

Liam's own personal journey mirrored this new-found balance. He'd always been driven and ambitious, sometimes to a fault, neglecting his own well-being in the pursuit of success. His relationship with Noah had taught him the importance of self-care, of setting boundaries, of prioritizing his mental and emotional health. He started incorporating regular exercise into his routine, dedicating time for meditation and reconnecting with old friends and hobbies, all of which helped to foster a more balanced approach to his life. This newfound equilibrium in his own life strengthened his ability to support Noah and their relationship.

Similarly, Noah's life became enriched by this newfound harmony. He had long struggled with a fear of vulnerability, a reluctance to fully embrace his own emotions. His relationship with Liam taught him the importance of self-expression, of allowing himself to feel and to share his feelings openly. He started expressing his creativity more freely, exploring new artistic avenues, and connecting with others on a deeper level. He found himself becoming more assertive and self-assured, a direct outcome of the trust and support he experienced in his partnership with Liam.

Their journey wasn't without its moments of friction, of course. They still had disagreements, still experienced moments of frustration and misunderstandings. But these moments were navigated with a newfound maturity, a shared understanding of the importance of open communication, mutual respect, and unwavering commitment to their partnership. They learned that true balance wasn't the absence of conflict, but the ability to navigate conflict constructively, to learn from their mistakes, and to emerge stronger and closer than before.

The house they shared, once a symbol of their burgeoning romance, now represented a sanctuary of mutual respect, individual growth, and shared joy. It was a space where they could each thrive, while simultaneously nurturing their deep and unwavering love for one another. It was a place where their individual identities flourished, enriching their shared life, and creating a deeply intimate and empowering partnership. Their story continued, not as a fairytale of seamless harmony, but as a testament to the beauty and strength found in building a life together, while still honoring the unique and precious individuality of each other. Their love was a beacon, a shining example of a balanced and thriving relationship, a love that blossomed not in spite of their differences, but because of them.

Chapter 5
Personal Growth

The following months unfolded like a carefully orchestrated dance, a delicate balance of shared moments and cherished solitude. Liam, emboldened by the newfound equilibrium in his life, decided to tackle a long-neglected passion: learning to play the guitar. He'd always admired musicians, the effortless grace with which they coaxed melodies from the strings, and now, with more time and a calmer mind, he felt ready to embark on this personal adventure. He enrolled in evening classes, finding a surprising sense of accomplishment in the slow, deliberate progress he made. The frustration of fumbling chords gave way to the satisfaction of mastering a simple riff, the clumsy strumming eventually transforming into a fluid, rhythmic melody. The quiet concentration required the focus on the task at hand provided a welcome respite from the demands of his work. Noah, ever supportive, would often sit beside him as he practiced, the silence punctuated only by the gentle plucking of strings and the occasional shared smile. He'd even surprised Liam with a beautiful vintage guitar, a thoughtful gift that reflected his understanding of Liam's newfound passion.

Meanwhile, Noah threw himself into his art with a renewed fervor. He'd always been a private individual, hesitant to share his work, but Liam's unwavering support had gradually eroded his insecurities. His upcoming exhibition loomed, a source of excitement and anxiety, but he embraced it instead of shrinking from the challenge. He spent hours in his studio, experimenting with new techniques and pushing the boundaries of his creative expression. He found a deeper connection to his art, a more profound understanding of his own artistic voice. He started attending workshops and collaborating with other artists, expanding his network and enriching his creative process. Liam eagerly awaited the unveiling of Noah's exhibition, proud of his partner's courage and artistic growth. He helped Noah set up the gallery, offering practical assistance and unwavering emotional support. The opening night was a resounding success, a testament to Noah's dedication and talent. Seeing Noah's beaming face, surrounded by admirers of his art, filled Liam with an overwhelming sense of pride and love.

Their individual pursuits weren't just separate activities; they became a source of mutual inspiration and support. Liam's newfound musical skills provided a soundtrack to their quiet evenings, while Noah's artistic explorations sparked lively conversations about creativity, expression, and the human condition. They'd often spend hours discussing their individual experiences, sharing insights and perspectives, strengthening their bond through a shared understanding of their personal growth. Liam started writing his own songs, inspired by his relationship with Noah, the melodies echoing the complexities of their shared journey. Noah, in turn, found new inspiration in Liam's music, integrating the emotive chords and rhythms into his paintings. Their lives intertwined, their individual passions enriching their shared world.

Their weekends were a tapestry of individual adventures and shared experiences. Liam rediscovered his love for hiking, exploring scenic trails and immersing himself in the beauty of nature. Noah, ever the introspective soul, enjoyed the quiet solitude, finding peace in the tranquil embrace of the wilderness. They'd often meet at a designated spot, sharing stories and observations from their respective journeys, the silence between them as meaningful as the words they exchanged. They explored local farmers' markets, Liam's enthusiasm for fresh produce balanced by Noah's appreciation for artisanal cheeses and loaves of bread. They attended theatre performances, Liam drawn to the vibrant energy of the stage, Noah captivated by the subtle nuances of human emotion portrayed on the stage. They even took a weekend trip to the coast, Liam reveling in the dynamism of the ocean waves, Noah finding solace in the quiet solitude of the beach. These experiences, while individually pursued, strengthened their bond, demonstrating the beauty of their shared journey.

Liam's personal growth extended beyond his hobbies. He started prioritizing his mental health incorporating mindfulness practices into his daily routine. He realized the importance of setting boundaries at work, learning to delegate tasks and prioritizing his own well-being. He rediscovered the joy of spending time with his friends, strengthening his social connections and building a supportive network. He even started volunteering at a local community center, finding fulfillment in giving back to the community. This holistic approach to self-care enriched his personal life and his relationship with Noah. He was a more present, patient, and understanding partner, better equipped to navigate the inevitable challenges of their relationship.

Noah's personal transformation was equally profound. He became more assertive, expressing his needs and desires more openly. He learned to trust his instincts, embracing his creative vision without fear of judgment. He connected with other artists, forming a supportive network that fostered his professional growth. He discovered a newfound confidence, a self-assurance that radiated from his very being. He was more emotionally available, sharing his vulnerability and anxieties without fear of rejection. He found his voice, both as an artist and as a person.

Their relationship evolved, becoming a space where individuality thrived alongside intimacy. They weren't just lovers but each other's greatest cheerleaders, their unwavering support fostering mutual growth and understanding. Their disagreements were no longer sources of conflict but opportunities for learning and growth, their differences enriching their shared life. They celebrated each other's successes, recognizing that each individual achievement strengthened their bond. They supported each other's dreams, providing encouragement and guidance without sacrificing their own aspirations.

One evening, sitting on their porch swing, the fireflies twinkling in the twilight, Liam looked at Noah, his heart overflowing with love and gratitude. He saw not just his lover, but a kindred spirit, a partner who had journeyed beside him, supporting his growth, encouraging his dreams, and accepting him unconditionally. Noah, in turn, felt an overwhelming sense of belonging, of being seen, understood, and loved for who he truly was. Their journey wasn't always easy, but it was beautiful, a testament to the power of individual growth within a deeply loving and supportive relationship framework. Their love story wasn't a fairytale; it was a real-life testament to the resilience of the human spirit, the transformative power of love, and the enduring strength of a partnership built on mutual respect, individual growth, and an unwavering commitment to each other. Their shared home wasn't just a house; it was a haven, a sanctuary, a testament to the beautiful tapestry of their intertwined lives. It was a space where their individual journeys converged, creating a rich and vibrant narrative of love, growth, and shared dreams.

The following spring brought with it a whirlwind of change. Feeling invigorated by his newfound musical proficiency and the stability of his relationship with Noah, Liam decided to apply for a promotion at his firm. He'd always been ambitious, but a sense of self-assurance, cultivated through his personal growth, propelled him forward. He poured over his application, crafting a compelling narrative that showcased not just his skills but also his evolved perspective – one that valued work-life balance and collaborative spirit. The interview process was nerve-wracking, but he approached it with a calmness he hadn't possessed before. He knew his value, understood his worth, and presented himself with confident humility. When it came, the promotion felt less like a victory and more like a natural progression, a testament to his hard work and personal evolution.

It came with increased responsibilities, a larger workload, and a significant salary increase, but Liam felt ready to embrace the challenge. He knew Noah would be there for him, offering unwavering support as he navigated this new phase of his professional life.

Noah, meanwhile, was experiencing a surge in his artistic career. His exhibition had garnered significant attention, leading to commissions and invitations to participate in group shows. He found himself juggling studio work, gallery meetings, and collaborations with other artists. This newfound success brought its own set of anxieties – managing deadlines, balancing creative freedom with client expectations, and navigating the complexities of the art world. But unlike before, he faced these challenges with a newfound resilience, a confidence born from his personal transformation. He sought out mentors, engaged in open dialogue with his peers, and learned to value constructive criticism. He understood that growth, like art itself, required both experimentation and refining, a delicate balance of embracing change and honoring the core principles of his creative vision.

The increased demands of their respective careers meant adjusting their routines. They had to consciously prioritize their time together, scheduling date nights and weekend getaways to maintain the intimacy that was the bedrock of their relationship. They learned to communicate effectively, sharing their anxieties and celebrating each other's successes. Their relationship became a safe haven, a space where they could be completely vulnerable and authentically themselves, understanding that change didn't diminish their bond but rather strengthened it.

A letter arrived one Saturday morning while Liam was practicing his guitar. It was an invitation to audition for a local band. The opportunity felt both exhilarating and daunting. He'd always dreamt of performing his music, but the thought of putting himself out there, exposing his vulnerability to a wider audience, was initially intimidating. He spent days agonizing over the decision, weighing the potential rewards against the risks of rejection. Noah, ever his supportive partner, encouraged him to embrace the challenge. He reminded Liam of his progress, of the confidence he'd cultivated, and of his undeniable talent. He helped Liam prepare for the audition, offering constructive feedback on his songs and encouraging him to believe in his abilities.

The audition was nerve-wracking, but Liam performed with a passion and conviction that surprised even himself. He poured his heart into his music, letting his emotions flow freely. The band members were impressed by his talent and his stage presence. The news of his acceptance into the band was met with exuberant joy and excitement. Liam had never felt so alive, so fulfilled.

With Liam's newfound musical engagement came a change in their shared lifestyle. Rehearsals took up a significant portion of his evenings, and weekend gigs occasionally disrupted their plans. While initially hesitant about the shift in their routine, Noah understood Liam's passion. He attended some of his performances, his pride radiating from his every gesture. He learned to adjust his schedule, ensuring he had time to support Liam's ambitions while pursuing his artistic endeavors. He became a dedicated member of Liam's unofficial support team, offering feedback, managing his social media, and generally being a rock.

Their relationship, far from being strained by these changes, evolved into a powerful partnership, a testament to their mutual respect and unwavering support. They learned to adapt, to compromise, and to celebrate each other's victories, no matter how small. They found a new rhythm in their lives, a harmonious balance between individual ambitions and shared dreams.

One day, Liam received a call from a record producer. They had seen him perform, and they were impressed. They offered him a contract. It was a dream come true, a culmination of years of hard work, dedication, and unwavering belief in himself. The news was met with a mixture of joy, disbelief, and a slight touch of overwhelming anxiety. Liam had always been afraid of success and what it might mean for his relationship, identity, and life. Noah, sensing his apprehension, gently reassured him. He reminded Liam of all the growth they'd experienced together, the strength of their bond, the unwavering support they had for each other.

The ensuing months were a whirlwind of studio sessions, songwriting, and the excitement of creating their debut album. They were busy, sometimes exhausted, but filled with an exhilaration that was both thrilling and humbling. Liam learned the value of teamwork, of collaboration, and of surrendering to the creative process. He also learned the importance of maintaining balance, prioritizing his mental health, and cherishing the intimacy of his relationship with Noah. They celebrated each milestone with a quiet dinner, a shared glass of wine, or a long, meaningful conversation.

Their lives continued to evolve, their journeys intersecting and enriching each other in unexpected ways. The changes they faced, though sometimes daunting, were never insurmountable. Their resilience, mutual support, and unwavering belief in each other were the cornerstones of their happiness, the foundation upon which they built their shared future. Their story wasn't just about navigating change; it was a testament to the enduring power of love, the resilience of the human spirit, and the beauty of a relationship forged in the fires of personal growth and mutual respect. It was a love story that defied expectations, transcended challenges, and found its rhythm in the symphony of their intertwined lives. They had embraced change, not as an adversary, but as a catalyst for growth, a force that propelled them toward a future brimming with promise and possibility. Their home, once simply a dwelling, had transformed into a sanctuary, a vibrant reflection of their individual passions and their shared dreams. It was a place where laughter mingled with quiet moments of reflection, where challenges were faced together and successes were celebrated with overflowing joy. Their story was a testament to the enduring power of love, a love that had weathered storms and celebrated triumphs, a love that had found its true strength not in the absence of change, but in the unwavering commitment to face it together, hand in hand, hearts entwined.

The following Christmas felt different. It wasn't just the twinkling lights adorning their apartment or the scent of pine needles and cinnamon filling the air. It was a deeper, more profound sense of contentment that permeated their celebration. Liam, basking in the glow of his burgeoning musical career, felt a gratitude he'd never experienced before. The record deal, initially a source of anxiety, had blossomed into an incredible journey of creativity and collaboration. He'd learned to manage the pressures of the music industry, prioritize his well-being, and maintain the balance between his professional aspirations and his personal life. He looked at Noah, his eyes reflecting the warm firelight, and felt an overwhelming sense of peace. Their relationship had become a sanctuary, a place where he could be completely himself, flaws and all.

Noah, too, felt a profound sense of fulfillment. His art career was flourishing, his work receiving critical acclaim and gaining a wider audience. He navigated the art world's complexities with grace and resilience, learning to value both his artistic vision and the constructive criticism that helped him refine his craft. He'd learned to manage his time effectively, balancing his own demanding schedule with his unwavering support for Liam's career. He understood the sacrifices and compromises required in a successful partnership and embraced them with open arms. He cherished the moments they shared, the quiet evenings spent together, the laughter that echoed through their apartment and the comforting presence of the other.

Their Christmas Eve was a testament to their growth. They didn't exchange lavish gifts; instead, they exchanged heartfelt promises, reaffirming their commitment to each other, their shared journey, and their enduring love. They cooked a simple meal together, their laughter filling the small kitchen as they reminisced about past Christmases, sharing stories and memories that had shaped their relationship. Later, curled up on the sofa, surrounded by twinkling lights and the crackling fireplace, they exchanged quiet moments of intimacy, sharing their hopes and dreams for the coming year. It was a celebration of their love, a testament to their resilience, and a promise of a future filled with shared joys and unwavering support.

Their first anniversary as a couple came in the spring. They marked the occasion with a quiet dinner at their favorite Italian restaurant. It wasn't a grand celebration; it was intimate, personal, and deeply meaningful. Over candlelit plates of pasta, they reminisced about their journey together, the challenges they'd overcome, and the growth they'd experienced. Liam confessed his initial apprehension about entering a serious relationship, admitting that he'd been afraid of commitment, of vulnerability. Noah, in turn, shared his struggles with self-doubt and insecurity, his past anxieties that had clouded his perception of his worthiness. The honest conversation stripped bare of pretense, served as a powerful affirmation of their journey together and the profound bond they had forged.

The following summer brought a trip to the coast, a much-needed escape from the whirlwind of their professional lives. Days were spent walking along the beach, the sound of crashing waves a soothing counterpoint to the silence between them, a silence filled with unspoken understanding. Evenings were filled with laughter, shared stories, and the quiet companionship that strengthened their connection. They didn't need constant conversation; their presence alone was enough, a comforting warmth that enveloped them both. It was in those quiet moments, away from the demands of their careers, that they found the space to reconnect, to nurture their relationship, and to strengthen their bond. They were not just lovers; they were partners, allies, best friends. Their love was not a fleeting emotion but a profound commitment, a testament to their shared journey of growth, resilience, and unwavering support.

One evening, nestled on the beach under a starlit sky, Liam confessed his fear of losing the spark, the initial passion that had ignited their relationship. He worried that the demands of their careers, the pressures of success, might eventually dull their connection. Noah, gently placing his hand over Liam's, reassured him. He explained that their love had evolved, deepened, and matured. The passion hadn't vanished; it had simply transformed, evolving into something deeper, more profound, and ultimately more enduring. It was a love that had weathered storms and celebrated triumphs, a love that had found its true strength in facing challenges together. It was a love that transcended fleeting emotions and embraced the enduring bond of friendship, loyalty, and unwavering support.

Their relationship continued to grow and evolve. They celebrated Liam's first album release with a small party, surrounded by close friends and family. The celebration wasn't about the music itself but about sharing a milestone in their journey, a testament to Liam's hard work, dedication, and Noah's unwavering support. They celebrated Noah's exhibition openings, sharing his pride in his artistic achievements. The joy wasn't just about the art; it was about their shared victories, mutual accomplishments and unfailing support for each other's dreams.

Years went by, marked by both significant events and small, everyday moments. Each holiday season brought its own set of traditions, carefully crafted over time, their personal history weaving into the fabric of their celebrations. Each anniversary was a chance to reflect on their journey, to acknowledge their growth, and to reaffirm their commitment to each other. They celebrated both big and small triumphs, learning to appreciate the subtle nuances of their shared lives, the quiet gestures of love that spoke volumes.

They navigated disagreements with greater maturity and understanding. They learned to communicate their needs and concerns openly and honestly, fostering an environment of trust and respect. They recognized that conflict wasn't a sign of failure; it was an opportunity for growth, a chance to deepen their understanding of each other, to refine their communication, and to strengthen their bond. Their arguments never led to destructive fights; instead, they were opportunities for reflection, leading to greater empathy and understanding.

Liam's musical career continued to flourish, leading to international tours and collaborations with renowned artists. Noah's art gained recognition worldwide, his work appearing in prestigious galleries and collections. Their individual successes only

amplified their shared journey; each achievement was celebrated as a collective victory, a testament to their mutual support and enduring love.

Through it all, their love remained the constant, a beacon of
stability and support in the midst of change and uncertainty.
Their relationship wasn't just a romantic partnership; it was a
deep friendship, a collaborative effort, a profound connection of
two souls intertwined, growing and evolving together, year after year. It was a testament to their maturity, resilience, and the
enduring power of love, a love that had survived and thrived in
the face of life's ever-changing currents. Their love story was a
testament to the belief that the best relationships are not those
that remain static, but those that grow, adapt, and evolve, side
by side, hand in hand, hearts entwined in a symphony of mutual
respect and unwavering commitment. And as the years unfolded, their love story continued a narrative woven with
threads of growth, understanding, and a love that only deepened with time.

The release of Liam's second album, "Echoes," was a whirlwind. Months of grueling studio sessions, fueled by late-night
coffees and the unwavering support of Noah, culminated in a
tangible masterpiece. The album launch party, held in a trendy
downtown loft, buzzed with energy. The air thrummed with the
anticipation of friends, family, and industry professionals, all ea-
ger to hear Liam's latest work. Noah, ever the artist's soul, had
designed the minimalistic yet elegant invitations, reflecting the
album's introspective yet powerful nature. He stood beside
Liam, a quiet pillar of strength, his hand resting reassuringly on

Liam's back as the crowd surged around them. Liam, usually brimming with nervous energy before a performance, felt a surprising calm. He knew, without a shadow of a doubt, that Noah's presence was his anchor, his grounding force in the storm of his burgeoning career.

The album was a critical success, earning Liam glowing reviews and propelling him further into the spotlight. But the success wasn't without its challenges. The relentless touring schedule, the pressure to maintain his creative momentum, and the constant demands of the industry began to take their toll. Liam found himself feeling increasingly isolated, the euphoria of success tinged with a growing sense of loneliness. He confided in Noah, his voice heavy with exhaustion and self-doubt. Sensing Liam's emotional fragility, Noah didn't offer platitudes or quick fixes. Instead, he listened patiently, offering words of understanding, empathy, and unwavering support. He helped Liam create a new schedule that prioritized self-care, integrating quiet evenings at home, relaxing baths, and even gentle yoga sessions into his hectic itinerary. He encouraged Liam to take breaks, reminding him that his well-being was paramount. He gently pushed him to set boundaries, reminding him that saying "no" to extra commitments wasn't a sign of weakness but a necessary act of self-preservation.

Meanwhile, Noah's career was also experiencing a period of significant growth. His latest collection of paintings, inspired by their shared journey and the emotional landscapes they'd navigated together, garnered immense attention at a prestigious art fair. Galleries from across the globe expressed interest, and

Noah was faced with the exciting yet daunting prospect of expanding his reach and influence. He shared the news with Liam, his heart brimming with excitement, but also aware of the challenges that lay ahead. Rather than being envious or overwhelmed by Noah's success, Liam celebrated it with the same enthusiasm and support that Noah always offered him. He actively helped Noah navigate the intricacies of the art world, offering his business acumen and practical advice, which Noah greatly appreciated. He attended gallery openings, enthusiastically conversing with curators and collectors, highlighting Noah's unique talent and vision. Their mutual support wasn't just about attending events; it was about a deep understanding of each other's goals and dreams.

One evening, after a particularly challenging day of negotiations with a demanding gallery owner, Noah arrived home feeling defeated and disheartened. He poured out his frustrations to Liam, his words laced with self-doubt. Liam, sensing Noah's vulnerability, responded with quiet reassurance. He gently reminded Noah of his extraordinary talent, unique artistic vision, and unwavering determination. He reminded Noah of the countless times he had overcome challenges, his spirit never broken, his creativity never dimmed. He celebrated Noah's resilience, emphasizing the importance of his perspective and vision in the art world. He helped Noah reframe the situation, focusing on the positive aspects of his career progression and the opportunities that lay ahead.

Their unwavering support for each other extended beyond their professional lives. They celebrated small victories together, from a perfectly cooked meal to a spontaneous dance session in their living room. They navigated setbacks with grace and understanding, offering each other comfort and solace during difficult times. They celebrated milestones in each other's families, lending support and creating lasting memories. They attended family events, supporting each other's personal lives and commitments. Noah gracefully attended Liam's family gatherings, showing respect for Liam's family values and traditions, and Liam offered the same support to Noah's family. This mutual respect and participation in each other's lives strengthened their bond significantly. They understood that love was about more than romantic gestures; it was about a shared life, a journey of growth and understanding, a bond built on mutual respect, support, and shared goals.

A year later, Liam and Noah stood side-by-side at the opening of Noah's first solo exhibition in New York City. The gallery was packed, a testament to Noah's growing reputation. Liam felt a surge of pride and affection amidst the throng of art critics and collectors. He watched as Noah, radiant and confident, engaged with visitors, discussing his work with passion and eloquence. Liam felt a sense of deep satisfaction, not just in Noah's success, but in the enduring strength of their relationship. Their love was a testament to unwavering support, a constant source of strength and motivation in their individual journeys. It was a love that nurtured growth, a love that fostered ambition, a love that celebrated achievements, big or small. Their love wasn't just a romantic connection; it was a partnership built on mutual respect, unwavering support, and a shared commitment to personal growth.

In the years that followed, their love story continued to unfold, a narrative woven with threads of shared triumphs, mutual support, and unwavering commitment. They learned to navigate life's challenges together, to celebrate each other's successes, and to provide each other with unfailing encouragement, support, and unconditional love. Their partnership transcended a simple romantic connection; it was a testament to their friendship, their commitment to shared dreams, and their unwavering belief in each other. Their journey demonstrated that true love was not just about sharing moments of joy but also about offering steadfast support during trials and tribulations, always there to lend a hand and celebrate victories, no matter how big or small. It was a love story for the ages, a testament to the power of unwavering support in fostering personal growth and strengthening an enduring bond. Their story wasn't merely a tale of romantic love, but a powerful illustration of the profound impact of steadfast friendship, loyalty, and unwavering support in building a life together. It was a testament to the enduring strength of their love, a love that continued to deepen and blossom year after year, rooted in a foundation of unwavering mutual support.

The crisp autumn air nipped at their cheeks as Liam and Noah strolled hand-in-hand through Central Park, the vibrant hues of the changing leaves mirroring the colorful tapestry of their shared life. Liam, his fingers intertwined with Noah's, felt a profound sense of contentment. The whirlwind of the past few years, the album releases, the art exhibitions, the navigating of demanding careers had brought them closer, forging a bond that felt unbreakable. He looked at Noah, his face illuminated by the late afternoon sun, and a warmth spread through his chest. This wasn't just a relationship; it was a partnership, a shared journey toward a future they had carefully and lovingly crafted together.

They had talked about their future often, those conversations woven into the fabric of their daily lives, as natural as breathing. It wasn't a formalized plan, a rigid checklist of goals, but rather a shared vision, a vibrant tapestry of dreams they were weaving together, thread by thread. Liam envisioned a life filled with music, continuing to create and share his art with the world. He saw himself traveling, performing in grand venues and intimate clubs alike, the roar of the crowd a familiar symphony. Yet, the thought of these moments wasn't exhilarating in isolation; it was the image of Noah beside him, his quiet support a constant presence, that truly fueled his ambition.

Noah, too, harbored aspirations beyond the canvas. He envisioned his art reaching a wider audience, his paintings adorning galleries across the globe, his unique style influencing a new generation of artists. He dreamt of teaching, sharing his passion and expertise with aspiring young talents, guiding them on their own artistic journeys. He pictured himself, years from now, lecturing at a prestigious art school, his classroom alive with creativity and the hum of inspired conversations. But this vision wasn't a solitary pursuit. The image of Liam in the audience, his proud smile a beacon of encouragement, was as vital to Noah's dreams as the brushstrokes on his canvases.

Their shared future wasn't just about individual accomplishments; it was about building a life together, a foundation of mutual respect and unwavering support. They spoke of a home, not just a house, but a sanctuary where laughter echoed in the hallways, music filled the air, and art adorned every wall, a testament to their shared passions and creativity. They imagined cozy nights spent by a crackling fireplace, surrounded by books and the comforting aroma of freshly brewed coffee, their fingers tracing each other's lines as they discussed their day, their dreams, and their shared vision for the future.

They talked about family, not just their own, but extending their love to encompass those they cherished. They envisioned large family gatherings filled with boisterous laughter, heartwarming stories, and the sweet scent of Grandma Rose's famous apple pie - a tradition Liam eagerly looked forward to sharing with Noah's family. They planned vacations, dreaming of exploring exotic lands together, soaking in the beauty of foreign cultures, and creating memories that would bind their hearts even more tightly. They talked about adopting a rescue dog, a furry companion to add to their lives, a loyal friend who would share in their joys and offer comfort during challenging times.

Their conversations weren't always about grand gestures; they were often filled with the quiet intimacy of everyday life. They discussed their favorite recipes, their plans for weekend gardening projects, their anxieties about upcoming deadlines.

They shared their vulnerabilities, their fears, and their aspirations, strengthening their bond with each honest exchange. These seemingly mundane discussions were the building blocks of their shared future, small moments that painted a picture of a life intertwined, a tapestry woven with threads of love, laughter, understanding, and unwavering support.

They understood that life wouldn't always be smooth sailing. There would be challenges, obstacles, and moments of doubt. But their conversations revealed a quiet confidence, a shared belief in their ability to overcome whatever life threw their way, as they always had. Their bond had been tested and refined by the crucible of career pressures and personal vulnerabilities, emerging stronger, more resilient, and more deeply rooted than ever before.

One evening, nestled on their couch, surrounded by scattered canvases and sheet music, Liam traced the lines of Noah's hand. "Remember that first gig in that tiny coffee shop?" he asked, a smile playing on his lips.

Noah chuckled, "How could I forget? Your voice was barely audible over the clatter of cups, but you were captivating. And my nerves were a complete wreck."

"And yet, here we are," Liam murmured, squeezing Noah's hand. "We made it."

"We did," Noah agreed, his gaze locking with Liam's. "And we'll keep making it… together."

Their shared future wasn't just a dream; it was a commitment, a conscious choice to build a life together, brick by brick, dream by dream. It was a testament to the power of their love, a love that wasn't just about romance, but about friendship, respect, shared ambitions, and an unwavering commitment to navigate life's journey side-by-side. It was a future painted not in bold strokes of grand gestures, but in the subtle nuances of shared laughter, quiet moments of intimacy, and the unwavering knowledge that they always had each other's backs.

The years that followed were a testament to their shared vision. Liam's music career continued to flourish, his songs touching hearts worldwide. Noah's art gained international recognition, his unique style celebrated by critics and collectors alike. Their home, a haven of creativity and love, filled with art, music, and the comforting presence of their rescued golden retriever, Gus, became a sanctuary from the storms of the outside world. They celebrated milestones together, from Liam's Grammy nomination to Noah's solo exhibition in the Louvre. They faced challenges with grace and resilience, their unwavering support for each other a constant source of strength.

They also carved out time for themselves, for quiet moments of reflection, for spontaneous adventures, and for simply being together. They found joy in the simple things: shared meals cooked together, long walks in the park and quiet evenings spent reading side-by-side. Their life wasn't perfect, but it was filled with a profound sense of purpose, a shared journey towards a future they had meticulously built, a future woven with the threads of love, laughter, shared dreams, and unwavering support. It was a future that promised not only individual success but a lifetime of happiness shared together, a testament to the enduring power of a love that transcended the boundaries of romance, blossoming into a deeply fulfilling partnership. Their shared future was a symphony of dreams, played in harmony, a masterpiece crafted by two souls intertwined, a testament to the strength of their bond and a beacon of hope for all who dared to dream of a love that could conquer all.

Chapter 6
A Love That Transcends

Their first public appearance as a couple at Liam's Grammy nomination ceremony was a calculated risk. Liam, ever the performer, felt the adrenaline surge as they walked the red carpet, hand in hand. Usually reserved, Noah had surprisingly embraced the moment, his hand nestled securely in Liam's, his smile a radiant counterpoint to Liam's practiced composure. The flashbulbs popped, capturing their image _ two men deeply in love, defying the unspoken rules that still lingered in certain corners of the industry. The whispers followed them, the subtle sidelong glances, the hushed conversations _ but Liam and Noah held their heads high, their love a shield against the barbs of prejudice. They had anticipated this, prepared for it, even practiced their confident smiles in the mirror the night before. What mattered was that they were together, their love visible, a testament to their strength and unity.

The subsequent weeks brought a wave of both support and criticism. Liam's largely progressive and accepting fanbase embraced Noah with open arms. Some articles celebrated their relationship as a symbol of progress, highlighting their success as a testament to love's resilience. Others, however, were less kind, their words laced with veiled homophobia and thinly disguised disapproval. Liam and Noah weathered the storm together, their shared experiences strengthening their bond. They refused to let negativity define them, instead using it as fuel to further solidify their love and commitment. They chose to focus on the positive and countless messages of support they received from fans worldwide who were inspired by their story.

Their relationship wasn't always a public spectacle. There were quiet moments, stolen kisses in dimly lit corners, hushed conversations over steaming mugs of coffee, laughter shared between just the two of them. These private moments were their anchors, grounding them in the midst of the public storm. These were the moments that truly mattered, the moments that reinforced their love beyond the glare of the spotlight.

One evening, at a lavish art gallery opening, Noah found himself surrounded by a group of art critics, their conversation a mixture of polite pleasantries and thinly veiled disdain. One critic, bolder than the rest, made a snide comment about Liam's "unconventional" choice of partner. Noah, usually mild-mannered, surprised himself with the fire that ignited in his eyes. He delivered a calm but firm response, explaining how Liam's support had been integral to his artistic success and how their love enriched, rather than diminished, his life and work. His eloquent defense silenced the room, leaving the critics momentarily speechless. The conversation shifted, and Noah found himself unexpectedly surrounded by a new wave of respect, both for his art and his outspoken defense of his love.

Their defiance wasn't always as eloquent or calculated. Sometimes, they simply held hands in public spaces, ignoring the stares, the whispers, and the occasional hateful comment. They chose to reclaim public spaces, to transform them from places of potential judgment into spaces of affirmation and love. Their simple act of holding hands became a quiet rebellion, a constant reminder that their love was real, valid, and worthy of celebration.

Their commitment extended beyond public displays. They consciously tried to integrate into each other's families and social circles. Liam's family, initially hesitant, embraced Noah with a warmth that surprised both men. Noah's family, already more open-minded, welcomed Liam with open arms. Family gatherings were filled with laughter and shared moments, proving that love could transcend even the deepest-rooted familial traditions and expectations. The gatherings were not only about acceptance, but also about the joy of building new traditions together, incorporating both families' unique histories and customs into their shared future.

Their journey wasn't always seamless. There were moments of doubt, of weariness from constantly battling prejudice. There were times when the weight of societal expectations pressed heavily upon them, threatening to stifle the flame of their love. But they always found their way back to each other, their bond resilient and unwavering. They learned to rely on each other to provide comfort and support in the face of adversity. They found strength in their shared vulnerabilities, embracing their imperfections and celebrating their unique strengths. Their love became a sanctuary, a haven from the storms of the outside world.

Their resilience inspired others. They received countless messages from fans and strangers alike, sharing their own stories of overcoming prejudice and discrimination. Liam and Noah's story became a symbol of hope, a reminder that love could prevail despite societal limitations. They became advocates for LGBTQ+ rights, using their platform to speak out against injustice and promote inclusivity. Their advocacy was not just about changing laws; it was about changing hearts and minds, one person at a time.

One particularly memorable evening, after a particularly grueling day of dealing with negative press, Liam and Noah sat on their balcony, the city lights twinkling before them. They held each other close, finding solace in the comforting weight of each other's presence. They spoke of their journey, of the challenges they had faced, and of the triumphs they had celebrated. Liam looked at Noah, the city lights reflecting in his eyes, and a profound sense of gratitude washed over him. He realized that their love wasn't just a personal triumph; it was a testament to the power of human connection, a beacon of hope in a world that often felt too divided.

They recognized that their fight was far from over and that there was still much work to be done in dismantling societal barriers and promoting acceptance. But they also knew that they had the strength, resilience, and unwavering support of each other to continue their journey. Their love was not merely a romance; it was a revolution, a quiet rebellion against the norms and a celebration of the power of human connection to transcend limitations and prejudices. It was a testament to their enduring love, which had survived but thrived amidst the challenges, emerging stronger and more radiant than ever before.

Their shared experiences transformed their relationship into something deeper, something richer than just romance. It became a testament to their unwavering commitment to each other, to their shared values, and to their resilience in the face of adversity. It was a love that challenged conventions, broke down barriers, and inspired countless others to embrace their true selves and fight for a more inclusive world. Their love story was not simply about two men falling in love; it was about the transformative power of love to conquer societal prejudices, foster understanding, and ignite a revolution of acceptance, one heart at a time. It was a love story for the ages, one that would continue to inspire and uplift, a legacy of love that transcended time, space, and societal boundaries. It was a love that truly overcame, a testament to the indomitable spirit of the human heart. Their story was a testament to the enduring power of love, proving that love, in its purest form, conquers all.

The following summer, Liam and Noah found themselves invited to speak at the annual Pride festival in their city. It wasn't just another appearance but a conscious decision to use their platform for something meaningful. The festival was a vibrant explosion of color, music, and energy, a powerful testament to the strength and resilience of the LGBTQ+ community. Liam, usually comfortable in the spotlight, felt a surge of nervous energy. This wasn't a glamorous red carpet event; this was about real people, sharing their stories, their struggles, and their triumphs. Noah, sensing his apprehension, squeezed his hand reassuringly. "We've got this," he whispered, his voice a steady anchor amidst the swirling chaos.

Their speech was short and heartfelt. Liam spoke first, his voice raw with emotion as he shared his journey of self-discovery and the fear he'd initially felt about publicly embracing his sexuality. He talked about the liberating power of love, the profound impact Noah had had on his life, and the importance of celebrating authenticity. Noah followed, his words elegant and powerful. He spoke about the importance of allyship, the need for empathy and understanding, and the urgent necessity to combat discrimination. They spoke not just as a couple, but as advocates, their words echoing across the square, resonating with the thousands of people gathered before them. The response was overwhelming. The crowd erupted in cheers, a wave of love and acceptance washing over them. People rushed forward to hug them, to express their gratitude, to share their own stories. It was a deeply moving experience, a powerful reminder of the strength that comes from collective solidarity.

Following the Pride festival, they accepted an invitation to speak at a diversity conference held at a prestigious university. This was a different audience – academics, students, and community leaders, all dedicated to fostering understanding and inclusivity. Liam and Noah chose to focus their message on the importance of intersectionality. They acknowledged that their experience as a successful gay couple, was not representative of the struggles faced by many others in the LGBTQ+ community, particularly those who faced multiple forms of marginalization. They used their platform to amplify the voices of other communities, to acknowledge and celebrate the rich tapestry of identities and experiences that made up the diverse spectrum of humanity.

Their appearance at the conference sparked a series of speaking engagements, each unique in its own context. They spoke at schools, engaging with young people, sharing their experiences and encouraging them to be themselves, regardless of societal pressures. They spoke at community centers, focusing on fostering understanding and combating hate speech. They spoke at corporate events, urging businesses to create more inclusive environments. With each engagement, they refined their message, learning to tailor their approach to resonate with diverse audiences. They began collaborating with organizations working to promote LGBTQ+ rights, mental health awareness, and racial equality. They used their influence not just to talk about inclusion but to create pathways to it actively.

One particular project deeply resonated with them. They partnered with a local arts organization to create a mural project that celebrated the diversity of their community. The mural, a vibrant explosion of color and texture, featured portraits of individuals from various backgrounds—different ethnicities, sexual orientations, genders, abilities, and ages, all united in their shared humanity. The community participated actively in the project, contributing ideas, sharing stories, and working alongside the artists to bring the mural to life. The mural unveiling was a joyful community event, a tangible symbol of the progress they were working towards.

Their work extended beyond public speaking and community projects. They used their social media platforms to share messages of hope and encourage dialogue. They engaged actively with their fans, answering questions, providing support, and amplifying other voices. They became role models, demonstrating through their actions the power of authenticity and empathy. They weren't afraid to challenge those who perpetuated prejudice, to call out injustices, and to fight for equality. Their public persona wasn't just about the glamour of their celebrity status; it was a vehicle for their activism.

But their activism wasn't solely confined to their public presence. In their quiet moments, their actions continued to reflect their commitment to diversity and inclusivity. Liam started mentoring young LGBTQ+ musicians, offering guidance, support, and opportunities. Noah used his artistic talents to collaborate with artists from diverse backgrounds, using their shared creativity to promote messages of hope and understanding. Their home became a haven for friends and family from all walks of life, a testament to the welcoming and inclusive environment they had consciously built.

They understood that celebrating diversity wasn't just about tolerance; it was about active participation and allyship. It was about challenging stereotypes and celebrating the rich tapestry of human experience. It was about seeing the inherent worth in every individual, regardless of their background or identity.

Their journey was far from over; they knew there was still much work to be done to achieve true equality and justice for all. But their commitment was unwavering, fuelled by their shared love, their deep empathy, and their unwavering belief in the power of human connection to create a more just and equitable world. Their legacy was shaping up to be one of profound influence, one that went far beyond the reach of their celebrity status. They were actively rewriting the narrative, one inclusive action, one empathetic conversation, one inspiring story at a time.

One evening, while watching the sunset from their balcony, Liam reflected on how far they'd come. The city lights mirrored the brilliance of the stars, creating a breathtaking panorama of light and color. He looked at Noah, his hand resting gently on his knee, and felt a profound sense of gratitude. Their relationship was a testament to the power of love, but it was also a catalyst for positive social change. It wasn't just a personal journey; it was a collective movement, a testament to the enduring human spirit's capacity for compassion, empathy, and the unwavering pursuit of justice for all. Their love story became a symbol of hope, a beacon that illuminated a path toward a more inclusive and equitable future, reminding others that love truly transcends all boundaries. Their celebration of diversity wasn't just an act; it was a lifestyle, a legacy, a commitment to a world where every individual could feel seen, heard, valued, and loved for exactly who they were. It was a future where differences were celebrated and common humanity shone brightly. Their journey was far from over, but each step they took, hand-in-hand, brought them closer to the world they envisioned, a world of genuine diversity, acceptance, and unconditional love.

The following months were a whirlwind. Their appearances at the Pride festival and the diversity conference had catapulted them into a new realm of influence. Requests for interviews, speaking engagements, and collaborations flooded their inboxes. It was exhilarating, exhausting, and deeply fulfilling all at once. They learned to navigate the demands of their newfound public platform, always mindful of the responsibility that came with it. They used their voices to champion causes close to their hearts, advocating for LGBTQ+ rights, mental health awareness, and racial justice.

One particularly poignant moment occurred during a visit to a high school in a rural town known for its conservative values. Liam and Noah had been invited to speak to a group of students as part of a school initiative focused on promoting inclusivity. The atmosphere was initially tense, with a palpable sense of apprehension hanging in the air. Some students were openly hostile, their faces reflecting a mixture of suspicion and disapproval. Others were simply curious, their eyes questioning, their expressions guarded.

Liam began by sharing his own story, his voice soft but firm. He recounted his struggles with self-acceptance, the isolation he'd felt growing up, and the fear he'd harbored about coming out. He spoke with honesty and vulnerability, his words weaving a tapestry of both pain and triumph. Noah listened attentively, his presence a reassuring beacon in the room.

As Liam's story unfolded, a shift began to occur. The initial hostility gradually faded, replaced by a quiet attentiveness. Students who had initially seemed dismissive began to lean forward, their expressions changing from skepticism to empathy. Liam spoke about the transformative power of love, about finding solace and strength in his relationship with Noah. He talked about the importance of self-acceptance the beauty of embracing one's authentic self despite societal pressures and expectations.

Noah followed Liam, his words eloquent and powerful. He spoke not just about acceptance, but about the active role everyone has to play in creating a more inclusive world. He emphasized the need for allyship, for empathy, and for standing up against discrimination. He urged the students to challenge prejudice, to be brave enough to speak out against injustice, and to be kind to themselves and to others.

The Q&A; session that followed was equally transformative. Students who had hesitated to engage at first began to share their own experiences, anxieties, and hopes for a more just and equitable future. The atmosphere in the room had completely changed. What had started as a potentially contentious event transformed into a powerful dialogue of mutual respect and understanding. A quiet ripple of hope and acceptance began to spread among the students, a collective acknowledgment that true change begins with self-reflection and courageous action.

Their visit to the high school was just one of many. They spoke at colleges, universities, community centers, and corporate events. With each appearance, they refined their message, tailoring it to the specific audience and context. They found themselves connecting with people from all walks of life, sharing stories, exchanging ideas, and inspiring hope.

One particularly meaningful experience was a visit to a children's hospital. Liam and Noah spent the afternoon sharing stories and playing games with young patients, many of whom were battling life-threatening illnesses. The joy they found in connecting with these children was immeasurable, a reminder of the simple power of human connection to transcend pain and hardship. They discovered that in those moments of shared vulnerability, the boundaries between celebrity and everyday life blurred, leaving only a shared experience of hope and compassion.

They continued to collaborate with various organizations, using their platform to amplify the voices of marginalized communities and to advocate for systemic change. They partnered with mental health organizations, focusing on raising awareness and reducing the stigma associated with mental illness. They collaborated with LGBTQ+ advocacy groups, working to advance equal rights and combat discrimination. Their commitment to social justice wasn't simply a public image; it was an integral part of their lives, woven into the fabric of their relationships and their daily actions.

Their social media presence became a powerful tool for connection and advocacy. They used their platforms to share stories, to raise awareness, and to inspire their followers. They were active in responding to comments and messages, engaging with their fans on a personal level. They became a source of comfort and inspiration for many young people grappling with questions of identity and belonging, offering words of encouragement and support. They provided a safe space for conversations about LGBTQ+ issues, mental health struggles, and racial inequality. Their online presence wasn't just about promoting their personal brand; it was a dynamic platform for building community and fostering social change.

Their journey, though deeply fulfilling, wasn't without its challenges. They faced criticism and backlash from some quarters and their work encountered resistance from those unwilling to embrace change. There were times when they felt overwhelmed, drained, and even disillusioned. But their shared love and commitment to their values provided an anchor amidst the storms.

One particular event highlighted the complexities of their influence. A controversial statement made by a public figure sparked intense debate and division. Liam and Noah were called upon to comment, and they carefully crafted a response that acknowledged the gravity of the situation and emphasized the importance of reasoned dialogue. While not explicitly condemning the public figure, their message stressed the urgent need for tolerance, empathy, and a commitment to creating an inclusive society. The response was mixed. Some praised them for their measured approach, while others criticized them for not being more forceful in their condemnation. The experience was a reminder of the delicate balance they had to navigate in their public role, a constant negotiation between advocacy and diplomacy.

Despite the challenges, Liam and Noah remained unwavering in their commitment to their cause. They understood that their platform was more than just a means of self-expression; it was a tool for positive social change. They continued to work tirelessly, inspiring others through their words and actions, striving to create a world where everyone felt seen, heard, valued, and loved. Their love story was not just a personal narrative. It was a testament to the power of compassion and the unwavering pursuit of a more just and equitable world. It was a story that resonated far beyond their individual lives, transforming into a beacon of hope and inspiration for countless others. Their legacy was one of empathy, inclusivity, and the unwavering belief in the transformative power of love – a love that truly transcends all boundaries.

The quiet hum of the evening filled their apartment, a comfortable silence punctuated only by the soft click of Noah's fingers on his laptop keyboard. Liam, curled up on the plush sofa, watched him, a gentle smile playing on his lips. The day had been a whirlwind – a flurry of emails, conference calls, and the frantic energy that seemed to perpetually surround their burgeoning public lives. But now, in the sanctuary of their shared space, the tension melted away. Noah looked up, catching Liam's gaze, and a slow, warm smile spread across his face.

"Rough day?" he asked, closing his laptop with a soft thud.

Liam nodded, stretching languidly. "Exhausting, but good. We connected with so many people today, students, activists, even a few hesitant parents who, by the end, were nodding along, getting it." He paused, a thoughtful expression clouding his features. "It's incredible, Noah. The impact we're having...it's almost overwhelming sometimes."

Noah rose and crossed the room, settling beside Liam on the sofa. He wrapped an arm around him, pulling Liam closer. The warmth of his embrace was a tangible comfort, a grounding force in the midst of the chaos. "Overwhelming, yes," Noah agreed softly, "but also deeply fulfilling. Remember that feeling in the high school? That shift in the room? That's what we're building, Liam. A ripple effect of understanding and acceptance."

Liam leaned into Noah's touch, the day's weight lifting slightly. He thought back to the many faces he'd seen – the scared faces of young people grappling with their identities, the weary faces of parents wrestling with societal pressures, and the hopeful faces of those who were finally finding their voice. Their journey hadn't been easy. They'd faced criticism, doubt, and moments of self-doubt. But through it all, their love had been the unwavering constant, a sturdy oak amidst a raging storm. It was the foundation upon which they built their platform, their message and their resilience.

"It's more than just speaking engagements, isn't it?" Liam murmured, his voice barely above a whisper. "It's about sharing our story, our truth, our love."

Noah kissed the top of his head, his touch gentle and reassuring. "Exactly. It's about showing the world what love truly looks like, vulnerable, messy, sometimes painful, but ultimately, incredibly powerful. A love that heals, that inspires, that transcends all boundaries."

Later that night, Liam found himself lost in thought after the city lights had dimmed and a comfortable silence settled over their apartment. He considered the moments of vulnerability they had shared, the tears they'd shed together, the fears they'd confronted hand-in-hand. These weren't just moments of weakness; they were moments of profound intimacy, where their love deepened, strengthened, and ultimately, healed.

He remembered a specific moment from their early days, a time when the weight of his past and the uncertainties of the future had nearly overwhelmed him. He'd curled up in a ball on their bed, consumed by a wave of anxiety, the fear of not being enough threatening to swallow him whole. Noah, ever the anchor, had simply sat beside him, his presence a silent reassurance, his hand resting gently on his back. He didn't offer platitudes or easy answers; he simply held space for Liam's pain, allowing him to grieve, to unravel, and to rebuild, piece by piece.

In those moments of shared vulnerability, Liam realized their love had truly blossomed. It wasn't the grand gestures or public pronouncements that defined their relationship; it was the quiet acts of kindness, the unspoken understanding, the unwavering support that sustained them through the storms. Their love was a refuge, a haven where they could be their authentic selves without judgment or reservation.

He traced the outline of Noah's sleeping form, the gentle rise and fall of his chest a comforting rhythm in the quiet room. He was everything Liam had ever longed for a confidante, a lover, a partner in crime, a beacon of hope in the darkness. He was the missing piece he hadn't known he was searching for, the missing piece that had, once found, transformed his world.

The following weeks were a blur of activity. They continued their work, their voices echoing in classrooms, conference halls, and online forums. They found themselves increasingly drawn to projects that focused on fostering empathy and understanding. They partnered with an organization dedicated to supporting LGBTQ+ youth experiencing homelessness, volunteering their time and resources to help provide shelter, food, and crucial emotional support.

While visiting a shelter one afternoon, Liam encountered a young woman named Sarah. Sarah was soft-spoken, her eyes haunted by a weariness far beyond her years. She shared her story, her voice trembling as she recounted her experiences of rejection, isolation, and the crushing weight of societal prejudice. Liam listened intently, feeling a deep empathy for her struggle. He shared his own story, his voice laced with vulnerability and understanding.

The conversation that followed was one of shared experiences, mutual respect, and burgeoning hope. Sarah, initially hesitant and withdrawn, began to open up, sharing her hopes and dreams. As she spoke, Liam saw a glimmer of light in her eyes, a spark of resilience reignited. Noah, observing from a distance, felt a profound sense of satisfaction. It wasn't just about the impact they were having on a broader scale; it was about these intimate moments of human connection, the quiet acts of empathy that made a profound difference in individual lives.

Their work extended beyond formal engagements. They used their social media platforms to amplify the voices of those who were often unheard, sharing stories of resilience, hope, and the transformative power of love. They created a safe space for vulnerable conversations, providing a platform for individuals to share their experiences without fear of judgment or ridicule.

One evening, as they scrolled through the comments on a recent post, they encountered a message that struck a particular chord. A young man named Daniel, who had been struggling with his sexuality and battling feelings of isolation, expressed his gratitude for their work. He wrote about finding solace and strength in their story, about feeling seen and understood for the first time in his life.

Liam and Noah felt an overwhelming wave of emotion. This was the ultimate validation of their efforts – the knowledge that they were making a tangible difference in the lives of others, that their love story was inspiring hope and providing strength to those who needed it most.

Their relationship was a testament to the enduring power of love, a beacon of hope in a world that often felt divided and uncertain. Their love was not just a personal narrative; it was a powerful testament to the healing power of connection, the transformative potential of vulnerability, and the boundless strength that could be found in shared experiences, mutual respect, and unwavering support. It was a love that not only sustained them through their own challenges but also provided strength and hope to countless others, proving that love, in its truest form, truly does transcend all boundaries. They had found strength in their love; in turn, their love had become a source of strength for the world around them. The journey had been demanding, challenging, even overwhelming at times, but the love they shared, deep and unwavering, was the compass guiding them through it all, a constant reminder that even in the face of adversity, love could conquer all.

The fire crackled merrily in the hearth, casting dancing shadows on the walls of their cozy cabin nestled deep within the Redwood National Park. Outside, the wind whispered secrets through the towering trees, a soothing lullaby to the quiet intimacy within. Liam, nestled against Noah's side, watched the flames flicker, his heart mirroring their gentle dance. The hectic pace of their lives, the relentless demands of their activism, had faded into a distant hum, replaced by the comforting silence of shared presence.

This was their sanctuary, a place where they could shed the weight of the world and simply be - Liam and Noah, two souls intertwined in a love that had weathered storms and emerged stronger, more resilient, and infinitely more profound. They had spent the last few days disconnected from the digital world, immersed in the breathtaking beauty of nature. The hikes through sun-dappled forests, the quiet evenings spent stargazing, the shared laughter echoing through the stillness, these were the moments that solidified their bond, reaffirming the unyielding strength of their love.

Liam reached out, his fingers tracing the line of Noah's jaw, feeling the soft stubble against his skin. Noah leaned into the touch, his eyes closing as he savored the simple intimacy. There was a deep-seated contentment in their silence, a profound understanding that transcended words. They had faced so much together - the skepticism, the criticism, the relentless pressure of the public eye. But through it all, their love had remained their unwavering compass, guiding them through the darkest nights and leading them toward a future brimming with hope.

He remembered the early days, the hesitant steps, the awkward silences, the fear of vulnerability. He thought of the countless nights they'd spent talking, sharing their dreams, their fears, their hopes. They had learned to embrace their vulnerabilities, find strength in their imperfections, and celebrate their differences. Their love wasn't a fairy tale; it was a testament to the resilience of the human spirit, a powerful narrative etched in moments of shared laughter, silent comfort, and unwavering support.

"Remember that first protest?" Noah asked, his voice a low murmur that resonated with the gentle crackling of the fire. "The one where we were so nervous we almost backed out?"

Liam chuckled, a warm sound that filled the quiet cabin. "How could I forget? We were practically shaking."

"But we did it," Noah said, squeezing Liam's hand. "Together. And that's what's always mattered, isn't it? We face everything together."

Their journey hadn't been easy. There were moments of doubt, moments of fear, moments when they questioned their ability to make a difference. But their love, their shared commitment to their cause, had propelled them forward, fuelling their resilience and strengthening their bond. They had learned to navigate the challenges of public life while protecting the sanctity of their private world. They understood the importance of carving out space for themselves, for their love, amidst the chaos and demands of their work.

The cabin, with its rustic charm and comforting warmth, had become a symbol of their resilience. It was a place where they could reconnect, where they could rediscover the quiet joys of being together, where they could recharge and prepare for whatever challenges lay ahead. It was a reminder that amidst the whirlwind of their public lives, their love remained their unwavering anchor, their safe haven.

They talked late into the night, their voices soft and intimate, sharing their dreams for the future. They spoke of expanding their work, reaching out to even more communities and creating more spaces for dialogue and understanding. They talked about traveling, exploring new places, creating new memories. They talked about their life together, the quiet joys and everyday moments that enriched their relationship, the small acts of kindness that sustained them.

They shared stories of the people they had helped, the lives they had touched, the impact they had made. These stories were a constant source of inspiration, a reminder of the power of their work and the significance of their shared journey. Each story was a testament to the transformative power of love, acceptance, and understanding, values that they championed in their public lives and private relationships.

The next morning, bathed in the soft glow of the rising sun, they embarked on a final hike, their hands intertwined, their hearts full. They walked in silence for a while, absorbing the beauty of the Redwood forest, its towering trees reaching towards the heavens. The serenity of nature, the majesty of the ancient trees seemed to reflect the enduring strength of their love.

As they reached a clearing, overlooking a breathtaking vista, Liam turned to Noah, his eyes filled with love and gratitude. "We've come so far," he said, his voice thick with emotion.

Noah smiled, his eyes reflecting the warmth of the sun. "And we'll go further, together."

Their love story wasn't just about them; it was about the impact they had on the world around them. It was about the lives they had touched, the hope they had inspired and the change they had initiated. It was a testament to the transformative power of love, a powerful narrative that continued to unfold, a beacon of hope in a world that often felt divided and uncertain.

Their love was a constant source of strength, a refuge from the storms of life. It was a love that nurtured, healed, and inspired. It was a love that not only sustained them but also gave strength to others, a testament to the boundless power of human connection, vulnerability, and unwavering support. It was a love that transcended all boundaries, a love that endured. And as they stood there, hand in hand, amidst the majestic beauty of the Redwood forest, they knew their love story was far from over. It was just beginning its next chapter, a chapter filled with promise, hope, and the unwavering certainty of a love that would continue to blossom, grow and endure forever. Their love was a legacy, a testament to the power of acceptance, and a beacon of hope for all who sought it. It was a love that was not only theirs, but a gift to the world. And that, they knew, was the most precious gift of all.